For my author family, who have pushed me to be better than I ever could be on my own.

A
SONGS OF LORALAN
ANTHOLOGY

THE LAND BUILT BY GIANTS

A.L. LORENSEN

CONTENTS

PREFACE

History forgotten
Is history repeated.
To this end
'Tis a bard's humble duty
To save us from ourselves.

'Neath our bluster and billow,
Our flourish and flounce,
Our purpose remains.
We bards protect stories
Of lives past and present.

Some shirk this holy mantle.
To those I bid farewell.
My lot is to know,
My lot is to teach,
The nearly forgotten hope in truth.

If truth offends

PREFACE

As so often it does
Make haste and depart.
For none shall escape
This bard's fiery tongue.

If truth you seek,
As so many have done,
Lean back,
Settle in,
And find it 'midst these golden tales.

-The Bard of Flames

THE ARCHITECTS OF ALCHILON

'Neath midwinter's floss
Adorned by heaven's clouded crown
Six giants slumber
The Architects of Alchilon

Before stars gilt the night
And daylight blossomed blue
These giants and their mother
Were all existence knew

Amidst the starless, endless sky
And cosmos swirling in loneliness
The giants prayed to their mother
To find others like themselves

Blessed by her embrace
The giants ventured from their mother's charge
To dull the ache of solitude
And become guardians of life, just as she was.

Others they did find
But not of their kin.
Instead Man, small, fragile,
But powerful for the fires within.

For Man the giants hung the sun in the heavens.
For man they planted waters in the earth.
Shaded trees and fruitful fields.
The Architects forged their sanctuary.

They created guardians of magic
To protect their precious Man.
They taught wisdom, love, and peace
And praised their mother in their hearts.

Love grew unfettered over days and centuries
Between Man and giants
Just as jealousy-forged chains
Imprisoned their mother's mind.

Who were they to forget her?
She who gave life?
They, who'd left with her blessing
Had abandoned her, forever.

Alone

Her great wings unfurled
And snuffed out the sky.
Just as her children had blessed Man with Day
Man would learn to fear her true Night.

Crops choked
Rivers ran dry

Animals fled
And Man faltered.

The Architects plead for the charges they loved.
Their words fell like saplings
'Gainst a withering storm.
And Mother Night cried for the children she'd lost.

The Architects wept
For their mother's suffering
And mourned the torment of Man.
A choice had to be made.

A choice to save one love
At the price of another.

To Mother Night the Architects turned their swords
Their tears as drops of dew so great
They carved great silver lakes of raging sorrow
In the battlefield they never wanted.

Mother Night's fury shook the heavens
And forged a storm that never faded.
Man had turned her blood against her.
And now that blood must be purged.

The first giant to fall
Fell in the North.
His mother's wings
Had claimed his heart.

The second fell
To the South at sea
Drowned in the depths

Of his Mother's tears.

The third and fourth
Fell in the West
Burned blind and mute
By their mother's fury

The fifth to fall
Fell in the East
Her head claimed
As her mother's victory.

The last she slayed
At the heart of the world
And laughed
As her body broke

Man watched in shattering grief.
Their saviors, teachers, protectors, friends
Had died for naught but useless creatures
Who could not even save themselves.

Man knelt for the Architects as their end loomed near.
Sang songs of memories made golden by love.
Their inner fires burned bright and true
For in their hearts, the Architects lived on.

Mother Night paused at man's simple gesture –
Took in the carnage at her feet.
Once, her children had gathered there
Alive and well to hear tales of life and love and hope.

Her scream rent the sky
Shattered it to pieces

As the weight of her sins
Stained the blood on her hands

The fractured sky fell
Leaving only threads in its place
"Stars" man would call them
When Mother Night's terror dissolved in time.

Six wounds – mortal wounds – etched into her chest
The mark of each child she'd slain.
Cursing and wailing, she fell from the sky
And vanished, with whispered vengeance, to return once
  again.

Man rebuilt what was broken
In the shadows of their giants.
Life sprung from their bodies
And thrived in their sleep.

Great forests from their chests
Great rivers from their eyes
Snowcapped peaks crowned their heads
As cities worshipped their feet.

Now, to some, they are naught but a mountain.
But in the warm breath of their breezes
The rumbling heartbeat of their cores
One can imagine they sleep, and wait.

To protect their love once more.

AS ONE

Who is man to magic?
A leaf beneath heavy boot?
Winter snow to summer's heat?
Or simple ash amidst the soot?

No, I say
Though some oppose
Man is far greater
Than those.

His magic lies within the heart
In fire and passion and brotherly bond.
He moves magic by mere presence alone
As a stone to the stillness of a pond.

What is magic to Man?
An artisan's tool?
Mere lights and color?
For a weary man, a stool?

No, I say
Though some oppose
Magic is far greater
Than those

Magic is Man's deepest wish come true.
Freedom, creativity, power, and life,
It moves man by existence alone
As a mother is moved by her child.

PRAYER OF REBIRTH

From sky's heav'nly fire,
Conceived in Earth's womb,
Came forth the Phoenix
Blessed with eternal life.

From fire to beings
From beings to ash
From ash to new life
We call our brothers forth

Take strength from the flames.
Take heart from the earth.
Take life from our words.
Arise and fly once more!

-Sung in phoenix clan revival ceremonies

REIGN OF FIRE

The dragon's just wrath
Rained upon the phoenix clan
And war descended

Man could not survive
Without the gift of magic
And perished in fire

The wisest of gods
Children of the Architects
Observed from their thrones

One day they would act
Put their brethren in their place
But not for decades

The earth caught ablaze
With hatred, ignorance, lies
And all simply watched

THE ANCIENT LAWS

'Midst the rubble
Of Man and Earth alike
The three races met
On the banks of heaven's fallen scales.

The race of gods
The dragon kin
And phoenix clan as one
To determine the welfare of Man.

"A pact must be made,"
The gods spoke to deafened ears,
"Limits to our boundless power
The world, ourselves, and Man to save."

Three days they counseled
Beside the Architects' fallen tears
Three laws they offered the Earth
To govern the lands of Alchilon.

"Magic may not be given to those without,"
The gods most loved by magic decreed,
"Lest a curse shall befall the land."

"Magic bound is magic beaten,"
The dragon-kin declared
Content no Man or magic could stay their might.

Upon ash-stained soil the phoenix stood
And severed the phoenix-clan's favor with Death
"The dead must remain with the dead."

Earth accepted the races' offerings
And took the bonds unto her soul.
With magic blessed and magic bound
The Ancient Laws were born.

FAREWELL

From sky's heav'nly fire,
Conceived in Earth's womb,
Came forth the Phoenix
Blessed with eternal life.

From fire to beings
From beings to ash
As ash you will stay
I lay you now to rest.

Find warmth in the flames
Find peace in the earth
Find love in my words
Rest and arise no more.

THE SORCERER AND THE SAINT

Gather 'round and delight
In the terrible plight
Of two friends torn apart
Before their friendship could start
All for the war 'twixt men and magic.

Banish your fears
And bend your ears.
The King may protest
But I humbly contest
That the stories worth hiding
Are the ones most worth telling.

On an isle far distant
Man was insistent
That magic brought nothing but anguish
And with their might they must vanquish
The sorcerers hidden midst their mountains.

As boys grew to men
They proved their ken
By slaying a sorcerer
Their malevolent others.
To them this murder was no sin
For a sorcerer, years ago, had slaughtered their kin.

And so to pursue this ultimate fight
A jailer's son went into the night.
He could not return without blood on his hands
He knew tradition's demands
Until he came upon his prize.

Caught in his trap of serpent root
Was not frothing, murderous brute
But a boy of a man
With a life and story and clan.
He could no more kill this sorcerer than he could a friend
And thus this man's boyhood came to an end.

He released the sorcerer and bound his wounds
And learned from him beneath countless moons
Friendship blossomed on barren soil
Washing clean their parents' toil.
But hate still festered in Man.

Man's son returned to his home
But life had changed within his bones.
By day he toiled as all men do
By night he worked by moon's silver hue
A jailer's son nurtured freedom.

He learned from his enemies –
The sorcerers hated for centuries.

He learned of magic, love, forgiveness
And friendship in all its richness.
He found love where Man found foe.
And Man had to know.

By night he crept back to his clan
No heed to the dangers of this plan.
Man must know the war had ended
And the nature of the lives they had upended.
His clan found him first, armed with torches and hate.

"Traitor!" they bellowed,
"Send him to his father's gallows!"
"Bewitched!" another cried.
The crowd parted aside
For no Man had spoken
Merely a sorcerer's devotion.

"I have enchanted him," the sorcerer lied.
"He does my bidding for the sake of my pride.
If someone must die, I am the monster you seek."
The mob's fear could not speak
As the sorcerer stood proud and strong and scared.

"He lies!" screamed the jailer's son.
He would not watch his friend undone.
"Everything I've done has been by choice!"
But Man refused to hear his weeping voice.
For a monster they had found alone
And for his ancestor's sins he must atone.

To the executioner they marched
The fire of vengeance sparked
The jailer's son, banished by the mob

Prayed to all and any gods above
To spare his friend; he'd pay the cost.

The gods stayed deaf to his pleas
As the sorcerer was forced to his knees
The executioner raised his bloodied axe
To mete out its doleful task.
The jailer's son could not endure
And all the world became a blur.

To the executioner he ran
And took the axe into his hand.
His clansmen turned to flee
As he broke the axe upon his knee.
"I will not let us murder one more soul!"

"We are not free of sin
We have killed our foe's innocent kin.
One sorcerer's evil hurt us dearly
But our sins stain us clearly.
When we continue to kill in the name of vengeance
We, not they, need repentance."

The mob stood in silence
Stilled by their history of violence.
Remorse guilted them to silent prayer
All save one, the jailer.
He would no more bear his son's enchantment.

Behind the crowd he drew his bow,
Nocked with its arrow of woe,
And set its course for the sorcerer's heart.
The cursed arrow found its mark.
The jailer's son fell to his end

For he had leapt to save his friend.

The sorcerer's anguish rent the night.
The mob gave up their fight.
Through shattered heart and veil of tears
The sorcerer prayed to any god t'would hear
To spare his friend; he'd pay the cost.

One god answered his echoed plea.
"Cast your trust with me."
Death appeared with hands outstretched
And runes upon their heads he etched.
"With one word I will bring him back
For love like yours the world lacks."

"The Ancient Laws have dulled my touch
I cannot do much.
Take this gift from me
And soon his life shall be
Restored, but only just."

"He shall be caught 'twixt life and death
Shall never take his final breath
'til you both shall choose that it is time
And he will once again be mine."
Death named his price.
The sorcerer begged for the rite.

Death placed his ring upon the dead man's hand
His death dissolved as bits of sand.
The jailer's son rose as promised
As summertime at its calmest.
And the two faced the crowd as brothers.

The mob abandoned their weapons
As guilt and shame beckoned
No more would they persecute their sorcerer brethren
Instead, their sins they would amend.
But tradition is difficult to break.

They chose to leave instead
Much the way it all had started.
The sorcerer and the jailer's son
Left together as one.
Bound now by friendship and Death's power
They vowed to cherish every hour.

With the sorcerers they'd sail to a new world
With flags and hopes unfurled.
They'd build a land where all could enter
A land where Man and Magic lived together.
They'd name their kingdom Loralan.

Through their joy and sorrow years
Death's price for life rang in their ears,
"When your time has come return my ring
And you shall evermore be as kings.
Fail, and my gift shall turn to vice
And you shall pay another price"

FAITHLESS

Greed consumed Death's gift.
Descendants lost its promise.
Death broke in madness.

CRAZY OLD MAPRIX

Young Malcolm Maprix
Lived in a tree
By the banks of the rivers three
It was there he dreamed of destiny
And girls as far as he could see.
No happier could he be.

But along came a spinster
What snatched up his sister.
And by golly that mister
He truly did miss her
And his ego did blister
So he left to capture the trickster.

Crazy old Maprix
Could not let the trickster be.
By golly he missed her
His sweet older sister
And left his homely tree.

So Malcolm Maprix
Set forth to the sea
A clever man still to be.
He planned to set his sister free
And break the spinster in the knee
Full deaf to her fearful pleas.

But his cleverness failed
Like a poor leaking pail
For the spinster had never set sail.
So he sat and he wailed
'Til the sun had paled
And the sailors had him jailed.

Crazy old Maprix
Clever, he'd failed to be.
His cleverness failed
So he sat and he wailed
On the beach of the lonely sea.

Now Malcolm Maprix
Cried woe is me
I shall never again be free.
I'll wash up by sea
With its salted debris
While and spinster and my sister flee.

But a princess did hear
Of his plight so dear.
She lent him her ear
And it drew up his tears.
From bars he disappeared
And they left for the old frontier.

Crazy old Maprix
In love he'd come to be.
She lent him her ear
And it drew up a tear
And from jail he chose to flee.

So Malcolm Maprix
Fled with his devotee
To the land of the spinster's tea.
But no spinster did he see
But a great and mighty she
Against Mother Night stood he.

With a hem and a haw
He fled from her maw
His fear rampaged raw.
His dear princess saw
And called out his flaw
And his anger she did draw.

Crazy old Maprix
Afeared as he should be.
He fled from her maw
And his dear princess saw
And he was angry as could be.

That Malcolm Maprix
Let out a decree
"Mother Night shall be killed by me!
Let the whole great world see
This legend to be
A man who lives in a tree."

The princess she pleaded

But her words when unheeded
A hero this world needed.
But out loud he conceded
With mercy his foe would be treated
But alas he was simply conceited.

Crazy old Maprix
A hero he meant to be.
The princess she pleaded
But he was conceited
And wanted the world to see.

Young Malcolm Maprix
Went his foe to see
As tall as a tree
And pretty as the sea
She could smite him like a flea.
But he had a plan, you see.

He talked of a treaty
His eyes dark and beady.
His motives were seedy
But his arguments meaty.
"My people are needy
So to you I come to entreaty."

Crazy old Maprix
Went to his foe to see.
He talked of a treaty
His motives all seedy
But clever for once he'd be.

This Malcolm Maprix
Was filled with glee

A. L. LORENSEN

When Mother Night agreed to be
Longstanding allies of godly decree
And shook his hand for all to see.
Her final act it would be.

He went and he killed her
And cheered for his murder.
The princess, he crossed her
Claimed her a monster.
He left with his sister
Told the princess he'd miss her.

Crazy old Maprix
Was filled with 'naught but glee.
He went and he killed her
Told the princess he'd miss her
And ran back home to his tree.

Old Malcolm Maprix
Claimed a sorcerer to be
When he got back home to his tree.
They all met him with glee
As he did magic for free
But he's still a murderer to me.

The princess behind
Made up her mind.
No longer would she be kind.
Maprix she would bind
His death warrant signed
To all suffering she would be blind.

Crazy old Maprix
A sorcerer he claimed to be.

Him she would bind
His death warrant signed
So he never again left his tree.

Crazy old Maprix
A sinner for all to see.
He never was clever
Used others as levers
And him I shall never be.

LULLABY

Hush now my child
My young meadowlark
Do not fear the dark
Your mother is watching,
My darling, my dear
And all will be will 'til you wake.

For I am the night
And I am the stars
That guard you my baby
Where'er you are
So sleep now in peace
Let all worries cease
For your mother shall ever stay near.

SHATTERED THREADS

"*Love flows through Loralan like blood through our veins,*" Val's mother told her as they stood on a grassy hillside, the night breeze ruffling their hair. "*It's the magic of this kingdom. If you look close enough, you will see its threads connecting everything around you.*"

Kana crouched next to her daughter, her eyes alight with warmth and power. Val gaped at her mother—at the blue threads of Kana's magic tying her to Val and every person in the village—with wonder.

"You see them, right?" Kana asked in a reverent whisper. "The threads that tie all of us together?"

Val reached out her pudgy, six-year-old hand and traced the strands. They glimmered like a thousand stars. The ground beneath their feet was a rainbow of glittering colors, so vibrant that Val had to squint to look. Val giggled. "I see them!"

None were as bright or pure as her mother's threads. A thick rope—intertwining strands of royal blue and a brighter one the color of lightning—tied Val's heart to her mother's. As the blue lights danced around her trailing fingers, Val tightened a fist around them and pulled experimentally.

Kana stiffened as if she had been struck. "Be careful, lark," she admonished with a small gasp of pain. "Pull too tightly and those will snap." She swept Val into her arms and laid her cheek against Val's dark hair. A long, glowing thread drifted from her back, casting a trail deep into the mountains.

"What's that one, Mama?" Val asked.

"Can you keep a secret?" Kana asked, poking Val's protruding belly.

Val folded her arms and pouted. "No," she said, disheartened.

Kana laughed. It was a rich sound that warmed Val from her head to her toes. "I think you can keep this one. It's very important to me." She looked Val in the eyes. "My best friend is a dragon."

Val's eyes grew wide. "Can I meet them?" she whispered.

Kana winked. "Maybe someday when you're older, and better at keeping secrets."

Val moaned with disappointment.

VAL STEPPED INTO THE TAVERN, her crisp Solacer's cape fluttering about her knees from the wind outside and a folded piece of parchment clutched in her hand. A few of the patrons cast her cursory glances, nodding in respect when they saw her cape and the kingdom's crest on it. Dim threads spread between them—the ties of acquaintances and neighbors. The tavern keep waved Val down, and then gestured his head to a corner of the room. Val nodded her thanks and turned.

She paused for a beat when she saw a figure huddled at the farthest, darkest table, watching her. Val almost wouldn't have noticed the person if not for the shock of long, platinum hair that hung in the girl's face. The girl didn't move. Just stared.

Val knit her brow warily and strode toward the girl. Her stomach fluttered uneasily. Her work often brought her into contact with people others would deem dangerous. The Ellonwyn Queen had wreaked havoc on the kingdom—sorcerers in particular. They had been hunted and captured or, if they were lucky, killed where they stood. All because their inherent magic had been perceived as a threat. That would drive anyone mad, and Val and the rest of the Solacer's had been specially trained to help those haunted souls with as much delicacy as possible. But the information she had on this case was particularly sparse. No name. No description. Just a letter asking for help.

And requesting Val in particular.

Val's neck prickled, but she approached. Her trepidation grew as she got closer. It was just a slip of a young woman, drowning in a dusty and torn dress three sizes too big for her. Her bare feet were cracked and bleeding. Smudges of dirt plastered her red, sunburnt skin, streaked with what looked like remnants of tears. Her golden hair was plastered to her scalp with sweat and filth—her expression gaunt and lifeless—and she silently regarded Val with dust-crusted eyes. The only thing remotely clean on her was a white feather tied to her belt. It gleamed and twinkled in the sunlight, long, broad, and perfect. A barbed, blindingly bright silver thread tied the girl to the feather.

Val sat across from the girl and placed the folded piece of parchment between them. "Did you write this letter?"

The girl didn't look at it, but continued to stare at Val with shocking, velvet blue eyes.

Val leaned forward, her elbows resting on the tavern table and her king's insignia glinting in the light from the tavern's modest hearth fire. The girl shied away from the sight of it.

Val inwardly winced to herself. No matter the odd feeling swirling in her gut, she still had to tread carefully. No sudden moves. No encroaching too close. This girl had been *hunted*, just like so many others. The scars would run deep for a long time to come. The vague uneasiness floating at the edge of Val's vision didn't matter.

"Will you tell me your name?" Val asked gently.

The girl turned away from Val, taking in the room at large. Her expression was vacant and lifeless, as if she didn't see any of it. "Are you Valeshta, daughter of Kana?" she asked in a soft, delicate voice, completely at odds with the state she was in.

Val narrowed her eyes, her heart sinking into her stomach as it panged with threads of grief. Why had this girl wanted to talk with *her*, and only her? "I am Valeshta Cormes, officer of the Solacer's, yes," she said slowly. "Am I not who you asked for when you sent your request for help?"

The girl's features darkened momentarily. "I never trust sorcerers to keep their word," she said with grim distaste. She tilted her head back to Val. Without a word, her hand shot out and clamped over Val's wrist.

Val didn't flinch—she had seen enough sorcerers driven mad by the Ellonwyn's persecution to know that flinching would often escalate things—but her magic flared in her eyes. Threads were easy to see, but seeing internal magic required more focus. Val's magic may have been weak in comparison to others, but it at least gave her an idea of who and what she was working with. It kept her alive.

The girl's figure burst with the fierce, bright light of magic. It was a roiling inferno of turmoil. Deep, unfocused, and dangerous. Val flinched before she could stop herself.

The girl grinned, her lip splitting and dribbling blood down her chin. "You can see them, can't you?" she asked in a whisper. "You have your mother's rare gift. You can see the threads. You can see the magic."

Val didn't say anything, but her heart thundered in her chest and a chill ran down her spine. Forcing her expression to stay neutral, she rested her hand over the girl's fingers. "Let go of me, please," she said quietly, amazed her voice didn't shake. "I'm here to help you."

The girl studied Val closely. Val felt like her soul was being scraped out of her body for examination.

The girl's grin widened, dead skin flaking off the corners of her mouth. "I believe you." She released Val and sat back, her bare feet scuffing against the floor. "What do you know about dragons?" she asked.

Val's mouth ran dry. Visions of her mother—of the long, blue thread that disappeared into the distance—played through her mind. How? There was no way this girl could have known...

But what other reason would she have to request Val as her Solacer?

"I know dragons are long dead," Val said curtly. She fell into her memorized Solacers script. "I'm not here for dragons. I'm here for *you*. Please let me know how I can best help you reintegrate into—"

"You can take me to the dragon your mother protected," the girl said eagerly, lurching across the table to reach for Val again. Val snatched her hands away. "That's how you can help me! You can see Kana's threads—you are the only sorcerer in all of Loralan that can."

"No." Val's answer came out short and abrupt, her hackles raising. This girl knew too much. Val couldn't begin to fathom how she had even gotten all this information, but it horrified her. "The kingdom's resources are already stretched thin in trying to repair the Ellonwyn Queen's damage done to sorcerers. If you intend to do nothing but waste the king's and my time, then I bid you good night."

The girl gaped blankly at Val, her fingers curling like rigid talons. It was several heartbeats before she spoke. "Valeshta, please. I need your help," she whispered. Distant thunder rumbled and Val furrowed her brows. It wasn't supposed to storm tonight. Val's magic roiled again, the air hissing and blistering around her with the girl's magic.

"I can only help you with shelter, food, clothing, and other necessities to build your life again," Val said flatly.

"You don't even know what I'm doing," the girl protested, jumping from the table with the squeal of chair legs. "I—"

"I can't help you with anything that involves dragons," Val barked, her jaw clenched. "They're gone, and that's the end of it."

"Even if I could save this kingdom?" The girl gave Val a pleading look. "Even if I could bring your mother back? Wouldn't you do *anything* to see her again?"

Val bristled, rage making her eyes burn. She ground her teeth. "My mother has no part in this discussion!"

Lightning cracked somewhere in the distance, but Val could have sworn she saw it arcing through the girl's eyes.

Val straightened, even as her body trembled beneath the shelter of her cape. "I leave in the morning. Think hard about what aid I can give you. If you have nothing new to add, then I will return to my duties. I will not answer your call again."

She stormed out of the tavern and slammed the door behind her.

VAL DREAMT of her mother that night. She remembered the feel of her mother's hair against her fingers when she would comb through it to wake her. She remembered the smell of her mother's perfume in its tiny bottle, and the way the sunlight would catch her mother's eyelashes, creating a crown of tiny sunbeams. How many times had they cuddled together as the sun skated across their faces and clouds trundled by outside the window? How many stories had Val heard as her mother braided her hair before bed?

The tears running down Val's face finally woke her, and she sat up in bed, leaning heavily against her bent knees and pressing her eyes into the palms of her hands. Of all the good work Val had done —finding homes and shelters for displaced sorcerers, locating sorcerers that had vanished during the Ellonwyn raids but had somehow survived, or tracking down the final resting place of those who had not—she had never been able to help her own mother. She hadn't had the courage to.

Val had felt their bond snap three years ago. She had collapsed from the pain that lanced through her heart. When she came to, the strand of magic connecting her to her mother had gone limp. Val had been inconsolable for months afterward.

The thread reached out into the far distance—into the mountains where her mother claimed her dragon lived—but Val had never followed it. She couldn't bear the thought of what was at the end.

Kana had been so *small.* Powerful in spirit, certainly, but age had turned her hair silver and worn spots on her skin. The weight of her wisdom and experience had curved her spine. Her confident strides had turned to determined shuffles, and her eyes had started to go milky at the edges. But, still, she had insisted that she go to protect the dragon that Val wasn't even sure existed. Kana had never taken her. Even with the winged Ellonwyn patrolling the kingdom for any sorcerer that dared to look their direction, Kana had insisted on leaving on her own. What could the winged people of the Ellonwyn want from an aging sorceress?

Val accidentally tore one of her blankets as she yanked it into place, her jaw clenched tight against her tears.

"The Pit *have* that dragon," she hissed to the darkness of her bedroom.

A shaft of moonlight filtered through her window and glinted off the bracelet she had taken off and left on the inn's wash table. The band was leather, but woven around a black scale with an iridescent sheen. Val sighed and padded over to it. She picked it up and ran her thumb over its surface, her thoughts straying to the girl in the tavern.

She didn't like the girl—didn't like the feeling she brought with her. She almost felt otherworldly, with her wide, staring eyes and uncanny stillness. Val easily outweighed and outsized her, but there was still something that frightened Val, much as she loathed to admit it. She wanted nothing to do with her.

What if I could bring your mother back?

Val frowned. The Ancient Laws were absolute. The dead must remain with the dead. The phoenixes had woven that law into the earth long before most histories had been written. But the surety in the girl's face—the power swirling through her—gave Val pause. Were the Laws absolute? Or was it that no one had dared challenge them before?

Val closed her eyes and breathed in memories, letting her mother's voice fill her with its warmth.

There is magic in the earth, Valeshta, just as surely as there is blood in our veins.

Val remembered her mother taking her hands and turning them palm upward in her lap.

And if you use that blood—that life—you will find the magic all around you.

Val turned her palms upward and breathed, tuning into the strength of her heart and the flow of blood through her veins. She breathed with its ebb and flow, letting the sensation wash over her. Tendrils of warmth seeped from her fingers, pressing gently into the space around her. Her mother's broken thread trailed from her heart into the distance, dim and ever-present. She sensed the furniture, bland and empty, the same as the walls and floor. Outside, the earth that had once been full of life was now faded and worn. Her magic pushed through the streets, sweeping through every corner of the town. The townsfolk still had some life in them, but only just. The war had taken its toll on the entire kingdom. Only one figure glowed, fierce and bright, with magic. The young woman at the tavern. Enough magic to be dangerous.

Perhaps enough magic to defy the gods.

Val opened her eyes, her magic returning to its resting spot in her chest. She sighed deeply and ran her thumb along the dragon scale again. "What do I do, ma?"

But she already knew the answer.

THE GIRL HADN'T MOVED from her corner spot in the tavern, despite all the other patrons having left and the tavern-keep wiping down the tables. He and Val had an understanding, so she was free to come and go as she pleased.

The girl's wide eyes fixed, unblinking, on Val. Val's unease returned ten-fold, and she stayed out of arm's reach, just in case.

"What do you want with the dragon?" Val asked tersely.

The girl's eyes narrowed in suspicion. "I have something to tell it."

Val compressed her lips. "If you're going about spouting nonsense of bringing back the dead, you have to give me something more than that."

The girl smiled so wide her lips cracked again. She touched the large white feather on her belt and a glaze of iridescent shimmers rippled across it from her fingertips. Her magic suddenly blazed to life, so bright and hot that Val had to take several steps back just to stand it. Her eyes went wide. She had never met someone that could project their magical presence like that.

"You believe you can break the Ancient Laws?" Val asked the girl, fighting to keep the awe out of her voice.

The girl nodded. She released her touch on the feather at her waist, and the press of her magic dimmed. "*If* you take me to the dragon."

Val looked away, rubbing her thumb over the dragon scale bracelet she had tucked into a pocket inside her cape. She let out a slow, shaking breath. Her mother would be furious with her. But at least she would be *alive*. She stuck out a hand. "I'll take you to the dragon."

Something flashed through the girl's eyes. Not quite human—not quite *sane*—and it made Val want to rescind her offer immediately. But the promise of hearing her mother's voice again was too great.

Val shook hands with the girl, her calluses scraping against the girl's raw sunburns.

The girl smiled at her as if she didn't register the pain. "I suppose you ought to know my name," she said. Thankfully, whatever Val had seen in her eyes had faded to a deep blue. "My name is Calliah."

THE NEXT MORNING, Val and Calliah stood next to each other with knapsacks provided by Val over their shoulders. They stared outside the town gate, where Kana's thread led. Seeing it made Val's breath hitch in her throat. Dread clawed its way up her spine. Her mother was at the end of that tendril of magic. In her mind, Val knew Kana was dead. But, her heart still wanted to cling to the slim hope that maybe her mother had been alive this whole time. This journey would be the end to that last sliver of hope.

Val cleared her throat to dislodge the lump there and plodded on.

"How did your mother find the dragon?" Calliah asked, bouncing on the balls of her bare feet as if she might otherwise combust with anxious energy.

"You ought to save your energy for the journey," Val said curtly, still battling with her emotions. "I imagine it'll be a few days' walk."

"I'll be fine." Calliah smiled at her. "Your mother's power was incredible. It's amazing you got such a rare gift, too! I don't know what I would have done without it."

Val ground her teeth. She didn't say anything.

"It's a pity you hadn't gone on this journey with your mother before. You could have just told me where to go and saved yourself the trip."

Those words slapped into Val like a few, well-timed backhands. Her ears rang.

Calliah shrugged, oblivious to Val's paled face. "Oh well. I suppose that just gives us more time to chat about what might have happened to her."

Val rounded on the younger woman, towering over her. "I agreed to take you to the dragon. I did *not* agree to your idle chatter."

Calliah reared back, affronted. "But isn't part of your duty to be friends with persecuted sorcerers? You may not have been powerful enough for the Ellonwyn to worry about, but I can assure you it was a diff—"

Val didn't let her finish. "This dragon hunt doesn't fall under my normal duties. I do not want to speak with you, *especially* about my mother. We will continue the rest of this journey in *silence.* Understood?"

A shadowy darkness spread across Calliah's face. Val's blood ran cold, but she didn't flinch.

Calliah looked at Val that way for a long time, her gaze freezing two holes of dread into Val's chest. Eventually, she nodded slowly. "Lead on, madam guide," she said with a husky growl.

Val nodded once in satisfaction and continued down the trail. She tried to ignore the girl behind her, but the hairs on the back of her neck stood on end for the rest of the day.

THE GIRL WOULD NOT STOP SINGING to herself. Ever since Val had stopped talking to her, Calliah had kept up a constant, semi-flat tune that set Val's teeth on edge.

> *Crazy old Maprix*
> *Went to his foe to see.*
> *He talked of a treaty*
> *His motives all seedy*
> *But clever for once he'd be.*
>
> *This Malcolm Maprix*
> *Was filled with glee*
> *When Mother Night agreed to be*
> *Longstanding allies of godly decree*
> *And shook his hand for all to see.*
> *Her final act it would be.*
>
> *He went and he killed her*
> *And cheered for his murder.*
> *The princess, he crossed her*
> *Claimed her a monster.*
> *He left with his sister*
> *Told the princess he'd miss her.*
>
> *Crazy old Maprix*
> *Was filled with 'naught but glee.*
> *He went and he killed her*
> *Told the princess he'd miss her*
> *And ran back home to his tree.*

Val recognized the song as a newer one that had swept through the local pubs after the death of the Ellonwyn Queen. It was a jaunty, rousing tune that Val had liked. However, after one too many verses from the girl—turned somehow haunting and mournful—Val wouldn't be happy until she never heard it again.

Only when they would stop for the night and lay out their bedrolls did Calliah's songs quiet to low murmurings. She would pull the long white feather off her belt and talk to it, brushing her fingers along the edges of it like she would a beloved pet. Val almost felt for her, but then snatches of Calliah's whispers would reach her.

"...I will bring you back."

"You were the light in midnight's darkness..."

"They have no idea what is waiting for them."

The words were spoken with such undercurrents of *deep* malice that they kept Val up late into the night, her fingers curled around a knife she had tucked away in her belt. She had worked with count-less broken sorcerers—ones that would lash out in fear and anger at the slightest breath. But none had ever truly terrified her as much as Calliah. Her madness seemed too complete. Calculated insanity.

Calliah never made a move toward Val, even though Val kept her body tensed for an attack. Eventually Val would drop off to sleep. Every morning when they woke, Val's stomach was in knots. Every step toward the creature her mother had loved so much felt like an act of betrayal. But, the dragon had been the reason for Kana's death, and Val had a score to settle with it. And even if she did change her mind, she had no idea how to renege on her promise without Calliah gutting her.

On their third night, Val saw where the threads of magic they had been following had snapped. Faded tendrils wafted down from the mountains, where they should have formed a continuous path with Val's end of the thread. Instead, the thread had frayed into erratic pieces, splattered like blood spots all over the trail and trees. Val's vision tunneled. Her steps faltered. The blue of her mother's magic flooded her vision.

Val staggered away a few paces. No. *No.* She wanted to run. She wanted to *fight.* She wanted to do *anything* that would make the scene vanish from her mind.

Val battled herself and eventually came back to the present, but her hands were clenched so tightly they shook. Sweat pooled on her temples. She couldn't draw a full breath. Haze swirled on the edges of her vision. She cut into the trees, just off the path. Just out of sight of where her mother had been murdered.

She dropped her pack off her shoulder and began unpacking without a word. The bracelet around her wrist felt like it might strangle her with its weight. Val expected Calliah to question why they were stopping when there was plenty of light and she had a gruff, barbed excuse ready. But, Calliah didn't protest. Instead, she crouched and began unpacking her own gear. She was so close to Val their shoulders brushed. There was a calming warmth to the touch.

"I know that look," Calliah said quietly, her voice the softest and most *sane* Val had ever heard it. She glanced at the girl, and her blue eyes were completely clear. No malice—no *madness.* Just a sorrowful understanding. "Is this where you lost your mother?"

Val wanted to snap at her, but the grief sat too heavy on her shoulders. So, she said nothing, and busied herself with smoothing out her bedroll.

"She was attacked by the Ellonwyn, wasn't she?"

Val couldn't speak past the lump of grief and anger in her throat.

Calliah was silent for a time, but Val felt her eyes on her back. "The Ellonwyn Queen didn't mean to hurt anyone," the girl finally said in earnest.

Val whirled, the movement so reflexive—so *angry*—that heat flared through her spine and up her neck. "*What?*"

If Calliah heard the acidic fury in Val's tone, she ignored it. "She was *sick.* Something drove her to madness. If someone just *helped* her, then all of this could have been fixed, and—"

"My mother is not the only one she took!" Val thundered, her jaw still clenched. She *would not* let tears fall down her face, but they were in her voice. "She took *everyone* with magic she deemed a threat. She took *children* from their mothers! Husbands and sisters and parents and anyone she could reach with her cursed wings. That's not *madness*. It's *murder!*"

Calliah reeled back this time, cringing away from Val's anger. "I'm telling you, she was *sick,*" She repeated, moisture welling in her eyes. "She needed *help*. She didn't deserve to be murdered! If we had just helped her, then she could have fixed—"

"You can't fix death!" Val roared, her eyes burning from the glow of her mother's broken, scattered magic. "This was a mistake to come here! I may want my mother back, but that is too great a price to pay if the Ellonwyn Queen finds a way to return. That monster deserved everything she got."

"You don't mean that." It wasn't a question or a statement. It was a threat—growling from the depths of Calliah's throat in a feral, unearthly sound. Her eyes had lost their vulnerable lucidity. Instead, they were bright and clouded again with something that sent a shiver down Val's spine. Val staggered back a few involuntary steps as Calliah rose to her full height. She was still smaller than Val, but her presence now loomed like a great beast overhead. She clutched the feather on her belt until her knuckles turned white. Magic arced and crackled around her in a blinding haze. "You know nothing of the slaughtered queen, and of the murderer deemed a hero. You know *nothing!* We are all but dogs to the fallen queen, and dogs are meant to *obey*." The command flooded all of Val's senses.

Val had no words. They lodged in her throat and refused to be spoken. Every other thought fled in the terror of Calliah's power. Val sat, because that was the only thing she could think to do. Her entire body shook—with rage, adrenaline, and fear. She had never seen a person flip so suddenly from sweet and soft-spoken to something so...*inhuman*. Whatever happened from here on out, Val knew she was no longer safe. She had *never* been safe. And she was a fool for it.

She expected Calliah to pace—to mutter, to scream, to sing her off-tune songs, do *anything*—but the girl only stood in perfect, statuesque silence, her eyes focused intently on a world Val couldn't see.

The lightning died around her, but sparks continued to leap from her clothes. She still clutched the white feather.

Val tucked herself deep into her bedroll facing Calliah, her eyes only partially closed so that she could watch her through her lashes.

"Remember your promise, Valeshta," Calliah's voice said, but Val couldn't tell if her mouth moved to form the words. "A sorcerer once broke a promise to me, and I won't let it happen again."

VAL DIDN'T SLEEP. Calliah kept her silent, unmoving watch until late into the night. Eventually her body seemed to give out. She crumpled where she stood and started lightly snoring.

Val stayed in her bedroll for another hour, watching Calliah and trying to figure out what to do. Crickets whirred in the trees, and fireflies bobbed along the trail of magic to where it seemed to disappear. That was where the cave had to be—the last stretch before reaching the dragon.

Val couldn't take Calliah up there. Whatever plans the girl had for the dragon could only be nefarious. And if that plan somehow managed to bring back the dead, it would spell doom for the rest of Loralan. But Val wasn't powerful enough to stop her. That had been made abundantly clear. She needed a way out of this mess. Fast.

As Val's thoughts tumbled in nonconstructive circles, growing grimmer with each moment, a song brushed her ears. Every thought stopped as her body clenched. She peeked at Calliah, but the girl was still snoring away, the feather cradled close to her like a doll. The song wasn't from her.

Val strained to hear the music. Was it one person? A group of people? Soldiers had been wandering in small units since the Ellonwyn Queen's death, searching for remnants of the winged people and driving them out of Loralan. If a group of soldiers was camped on the mountainside, they might be able to help. As Val listened, she saw faint traces of gold wend their way through the trees, curling and bobbing in time with the music. *Magic.*

Val hesitated for a moment. Approaching unknown sorcerers was an easy way to wind up seriously injured. Or worse.

Val glanced at Calliah again, who looked peaceful but other-worldly in the mottled moonlight. She'd rather chance her luck on an unknown devil than the one she had here.

Val eased her way out of her bedroll, grimacing at her rustling blankets and watching Calliah for any signs of movement. Val slipped her boots on, heart pounding in her mouth. She refused to think about what would happen if Calliah caught her. She had made her choice, and she would live with the consequences.

Chills still ran down her spine as she snuck away.

No matter how much her mind screamed at her to run, Val clenched her teeth and continued forward cautiously. She would not be a slave to fear. A mad dash through the trees would make too much noise and leave an obvious trail behind her. She would keep her head. She had to—no matter what her trembling limbs said otherwise.

It surprised Val how long it took her to follow the magic to its source. Sound shouldn't have carried as far as it had unless it was inexplicably tied to the magic or was purposefully being projected. Val didn't like the feeling of being lured into a trap, but she had no other choice. She touched her mother's bracelet for good luck—the dragon scale cool and smooth beneath her fingers—and pressed on.

Eventually, firelight came into view, warm and soft against the cold shadows of the trees. A woman's voice carried to Val, accompanied by plucked lute chords. The sound of the woman's song was rich and inviting—a soothing balm to the fear Val had been stifling. Val still approached with caution, unwilling to put her life in someone else's hands again. Calliah's wretched, growling voice still haunted her.

Keeping to the shadows and moving only when necessary—just as she had done while hunting game throughout her childhood—Val maneuvered herself into a vantage point. From behind a wide oak, she peered out at the singing woman.

The woman had tucked herself against a large, mossy rock, staring into the stars as she sang and twanged the lute in her lap. Her stockinged feet rested near her fire, which leapt and danced merrily in time with her song. The shadows it cast trailed across the woman like puppets, highlighting a large, jagged scar that crossed the bridge of her nose and both eyelids. Other than that single scar, there wasn't anything of note about the woman. She was young and of average build—someone that Val could have passed a thousand times in a crowd and never noticed.

The woman ended her song and smiled at her lute, turning one of the pegs at the end of its neck to adjust a string until she was satisfied. "Should we play something our guest will know?" she asked it.

Val froze, dread clawing up her throat.

The woman didn't wait for a response from her lute, but began to strum a soft, crooning song.

> *Hush now my child*
> *My young meadowlark*
> *Do not fear the dark*
> *Your mother is watching,*
> *My darling, my dear*
> *And all will be well 'til you wake.*

If an arrow had struck Val in the heart at that moment, it would have hurt less. Tears sprang to her eyes. In this—the place her mother had visited so often and died in—her mother's lullaby resonated deep within her bones and tore through her heart. Before she could stop herself, she stepped into the firelight, all caution and logic dismissed. No one could mean her harm when they sang those words.

The woman smiled at her but kept singing. She motioned with her head for Val to sit next to her by the fire. Val did so without question, her cheeks wet. She joined in the song, her voice thick and tremulous.

> *For I am the night*
> *And I am the stars*
> *That guard you my baby*
> *Where'er you are*
> *So sleep now in peace*
> *Let all worries cease*
> *For your mother shall ever stay near.*

Every word was like a stitch over a wound Val didn't realize she had left open. They ached, but there was healing in them, too. The gold-tinged music swirled past Val, twisting through the forest and awakening a deep blue glow. *Kana's* glow.

I love you, Val, her mother's voice whispered. Val covered her mouth as a sob hitched in her chest, more tears streaking down her cheeks. She never thought she would hear that voice again.

I made a choice to protect my friend, her mother said. *My choices are not your burden to bear. I love you so, so much.*

Val closed her eyes and let the words sweep over her. With every breath, she felt her mother's arms wrap around her—felt her heartbeat beside her own and the fizz Kana's magic always carried with it when she was near. Val didn't feel tethered to the earth anymore. Instead, she was enveloped, wholly and completely, in her mother's love. Free and light and complete.

The song ended, and the weightlessness faded, but the overflow of emotions remained in Val's chest, warm and comforting. She took a breath as if it were her first—the air clear and bracing and *alive*. When Val opened her eyes, the other woman was watching her with a softness that could have been an embrace. Val felt no shame for the tears that lingered on her cheeks.

"Who are you?"

The woman smiled. "Just a bard." Val got the impression that was the only information she would get on the matter. The bard leaned forward. "Your mother helped me write that song years ago," her smile fell, taking in Val's tears. "How long ago did you lose her?"

"A few years," Val said, amazed at how easy it was to talk with this woman whose eyes seemed as old as the mountains themselves. "Did you know her well?"

"Enough to know that she was never to be crossed, and that you were her whole world." She smiled sadly at Val. "We crossed paths frequently on our way to see an old friend." She motioned to the top of the mountain.

Val shook her head. "Seems everyone but me made that trek."

The bard chuckled. "Your mother made the treks. I try, but always stop before reaching the top." She tightened her grip around the lute, the strings plinking sadly. She didn't elaborate any further than that. Her eyes glossed over for a moment, but then she blinked, and they came back into focus. "Are you here to take up your mother's self-appointed mantle?"

A knot twisted itself in Val's gut, growing with a feeling as dark and hollow as Calliah's presence. "No," she said. She glanced up the mountain. Her mother's magic burned bright in the dark. She didn't know how many times her mother had walked up and down that mountain path, but she knew one thing. It was time the dragon made its own path. She knew what she had to do. It was the only way.

Val turned to the bard. "Thank you for the song. I don't know what kind of magic you put into it, but it was what I needed." She stood and faced the mountain. She had an hour—two at most—before the sky would start to lighten and wake Calliah. She had to work fast.

The bard stood with her, following her gaze up the mountain. "Do you need help?" she asked Val. There was an odd sort of weight to the question. It was more than just a token gesture. It rang with the idea that "help" could be many things.

Val shook her head. "Thank you, but no. This is my lot to finish."

The bard frowned but nodded. Val left her and trekked the rest of the way up the mountain, guided by the light of her mother's magic.

THE END of the trail was exactly as Val had anticipated it to be. A tumble of rocks, large, foreboding, and seemingly impenetrable. But, when she followed her mother's magic around one particular angle, a cavern entrance appeared between two sheer walls. Taking a bracing breath, she made her way inside.

The cavern was deep, but shafts of natural light seeped in through cracks in the cavern walls, lighting her path. Daylight was already breaking. She didn't know how much time she would have before Calliah made her way up the mountain.

As Val drew deeper into the caves, blasts of warm air swept past her in regular bursts, carrying with them the smell of sulfur and dust. It wasn't until the sun crested over the mountain and flooded through a natural skylight that she realized the gusts were not rumblings from the depths of the earth, but the deep breaths of a sleeping dragon.

Its form was massive, filling nearly the entire cavern like a cat curled up in a crate. Its black hide shimmered like iridescent obsidian in the light, rising and falling like the tide with every breath. Its head was as long as Val was tall, with horns curving elegantly away from the crown, and rested on its large, wicked talons. Nestled close to the dragon's ribs were the skeletal remains of a smaller dragon, and within that was a nest of five large eggs, each glowing as the light touched them. A thick, broken thread wafted forlornly between the dragon and the skeleton, but blinding threads wrapped around each of the eggs from its heart. Magic swirled within the eggs in a riot of colors, and Val let out a gasp before she could stop herself. Sweet Sister Earth, they were still *alive!*

The black dragon stirred, flexing its talons and raking deep furrows in the dirt.

Is that you, Kana? his voice rumbled in Val's mind, deep and gravelly. He opened one silver eye, milky with age. *I've been wondering what I've done to offend you.* Thundering sound came from the dragon's throat in short, quick bursts, and with a start, Val realized the dragon was *laughing.*

"H-hello," she choked out past the dryness in her mouth. "I'm sorry, but I—I'm not Kana. She died."

The dragon's laughing stilled. *Dead?* A mournful sound tumbled from his jaws. *Death is cruel, to make me watch so many loved ones come and go and leave me behind in this world. I am so lonely, but still he will not claim me,* the dragon keened, his tail lashing fretfully against the cavern walls. Rubble rained down, and the skylight grew larger as its edges crumbled. Val threw her hands over her head to shield herself. The bracelet flashed in the light.

The dragon's writhing stopped. He gazed, transfixed, at the bracelet. He swung his head slowly toward Val, sniffing deeply. *You carry the mark of my friend,* he said as he peered at the bracelet. *And you smell of Kana. Are you the Valeshta I have heard so much about?*

Val gaped at the dragon. "Ma spoke of me? To *you?*"

More laughter from the dragon. *You stand in the presence of the last of the great dragons, and* that *is your question?* The dragon settled low, his head resting on the ground so his eyes could be level with hers. *Yes, Valeshta, I know many things about you. You were your mother's treasure, and she doted over you as fiercely as any dragon over its hoard.* He stretched one of his dark wings over his clutch of eggs, drawing them protectively closer. *I am Shastrith,* he said. *Stories of you kept me company through what otherwise would have been many dark, lonely years. It is an honor to finally meet you.*

Val wanted to speak of her mother—ask what stories she told and hear his stories of Kana—but she knew what was making its way up the mountain.

"Shastrith, I would stay here for days on end to hear stories about my mother, but someone is coming for you. I don't know what their intentions are, but I know they're not good." She placed her hand on his snout, his scales warm and smooth beneath her palm. "You have to leave."

Shastrith reared his head back, almost panicked. *I cannot,* he said, his tail curling tightly around the skeletal dragon. *My treasures are here. I cannot leave my mate and clutch.*

Val looked at the dragon remains, her heart breaking. "That's your mate?"

A small whimper sounded from Shastrith.

Val was reminded of her mother's bed at home, untouched. A physical shrine to everything she had lost. "Shastrith, I—" she swallowed the lump in her throat. "You can't sit in the dark forever. You have spent your time mourning. I know the loss will never truly be gone, but wouldn't your mate want you to be safe? To be happy?"

My mate and I wanted many things, Shastrith said bitterly. *But we don't always get what we want.*

"Shastrith, *please.* You are my mother's dearest friend. *Please* let me help you. We'll take the eggs somewhere safe, and—"

"*Nowhere* is safe for you anymore."

Val was blown back into the cavern wall, smashing her shoulder. She tried to draw herself back up, but she couldn't breathe. Air currents swirled around her, sucking the oxygen away from her lungs. She gasped and clawed at her throat, but couldn't draw breath.

"You sorcerers dare lie to me *again?*"

Through hazy vision, Val saw Calliah's tiny form.

"I warned you, Valeshta!" the girl cried, her soft voice shrill and dark. "I told you what would happen! And unlike you, I keep my promises!"

Val's soul felt detached from her body, swirling high over her head as she watched herself die.

Shastrith roared and flung his tail at Calliah. Calliah stopped him from flattening her with a burst of magic, but that distracted her away from Val. The winds died, and Val could *breathe* again.

"I am not your enemy!" Calliah shouted at Shastrith. "I'm here to make a deal!"

We do not make deals with those that hurt our kin, Shastrith seethed, his tail lashing across the cavern and his wings bristling.

Kin? Val thought, her heart blooming with warmth.

"What if someone you viewed as kin betrayed you?"

Shastrith's tail stilled. Smoke billowed from his nose, but his eyes had fixed solely on Calliah. *What is it you seek from the last of the drag-ons?* he asked, a low growl forcing its way from his chest.

Val picked herself up, her body screaming, and inched her way out of Calliah's eyesight toward the dragon eggs. "Shastrith, you can't listen to this girl," she hissed. "She's not right in the head."

But Shastrith either didn't hear her or decided to ignore her.

Before Val could get completely out of view, Calliah turned her gaze back on her. She spat something in a language Val didn't under-stand, and Val's body seized up, not hurt, but unable to move. Val's eyes widened and dread seeped down her spine.

Calliah's grin returned—devoid of everything except pure, horri-fying satisfaction. "I seek what is mine," she said to Shastrith. "I seek what was taken."

Even with the inhuman look on Calliah's face, Val recognized the very human emotion in her voice. Loss. Grief. The sound of someone whose loved one had been ripped from them too soon. Val knew that voice well.

It seemed Shastrith did as well. A great shudder ran the length of his body. *What you wish for I cannot give,* he said. *One cannot steal what is Death's.* His tail twined with the skeletal tail beside him.

Calliah drew herself to her full height, her chin tilted regally. "I aim to rectify the phoenix' mistake," she said with full confidence. "Your power will be my first great step toward that goal." A sneer spread across her face. "Laws written by imperfect gods must wallow in imperfection by nature."

Shastrith considered her for a long moment. Val's heart pounded in her throat as she silently begged the dragon to banish the girl from the cave.

But he didn't. Instead, he considered her, his silver eyes gleaming in the stray beams of light. *What will I receive in exchange for my power?*

Val's stomach dropped. No. *No!* "Shastrith, don't listen to her!" she hissed again.

Calliah drew her feather from her belt, stroking it carefully. "New life," she said.

I have lived too many, Shastrith replied wearily.

Calliah's smile faltered slightly. "Dominion over all Man, then."

Shastrith let out a snort that made smoke plume from his nostrils. *What use have I for Man?*

Val's panic began to settle. She should have trusted the dragon. Her mother did not abide fools, and it seemed Shastrith was no exception. He knew exactly what he was doing.

Calliah's confidence seemed to be shaken. Her grin dropped entirely from her face. "Vengeance upon your foes," she said, beginning to sound desperate.

Death has embraced them long ago, Shastrith said, his tail lashing again.

Despite another negative answer, Calliah's grin returned, her eyes glittering with glee. "Save for one," she said quietly.

Shastrith's body went still, as if every muscle in his body had been seized with the same magic Val's had been. *What do you mean?* he asked, his words slow and dangerous.

"The last phoenix lives on," Calliah said in triumph.

The words hung silently in the air, like blades strung from the ceiling. Val didn't breathe. Shastrith didn't move. Calliah smiled.

So, Shastrith finally said in a quiet voice that hissed with bitterness. *Death has played his favorites.*

The roar of fury that tore from Shastrith's chest shook the foundations of the mountain itself. Val's heart jumped into her throat, and her vision went dark in panic. Her ears ached. The spell over Val broke, and she collapsed. She cupped her hands over her ears.

"Shastrith, your eggs!" she shouted desperately.

They do not matter anymore! Shastrith bellowed, shrieks of rage and anguish ricocheting through the cave. *Nothing matters when Death refuses to follow the Laws! I will have my justice!*

Shastrith thrashed in fury. Clenching her jaw, Val threw herself over the eggs, which leapt and trembled in their nest. Rocks and debris clattered against her back, but she didn't move. "Shastrith, *calm down!*" she barked, but the dragon didn't hear her. A boulder fell from the ceiling and smashed the skeletal dragon's skull beneath it. The sound of it shattered Val's heart.

Calliah approached the dragon, her eyes wide with excitement as she drew the feather from her belt. She whispered to it in a hissing, guttural language, and both it and her eyes glowed. With a grin that tore at the corners of her mouth, the girl looked up at the enraged dragon. "Will you give me your power to rectify this injustice?"

I will burn those phoenixes to less than ash! Fire leapt from his mouth.

Calliah grinned and took up her chant again, the feather glowing until it was blinding to look at. Shastrith writhed and howled in pain. Val shut her eyes and curled herself tighter around the eggs as Shastrith's tail flailed in deadly arcs. Her ears rang, and her gut clenched at the realization that she couldn't save her mother's friend. The guilt twisted through her insides, more painful than the rocks battering against her body. "I'm sorry," she whispered—to Shastrith, to her mother, and to the eggs she knew would be crushed as the mountain fell around them.

"Never be sorry for trying to do right," a voice said to her; fierce and quiet but somehow carrying to her through the chaos.

Val whipped her head around and saw the bard crouched beside her, tucked out of the way of Shastrith's and Calliah's eyesight. Her skin and eyes had an odd golden glow to them, and she radiated heat.

Despite everything happening around her, an odd sort of comfort settled over Val. "What in *Sister* Earth are you doing here?"

The bard didn't answer, but instead looked Val in the eyes with deep intensity. "Do you need help?"

"What do you *mean* do I need help? I'm about to be crushed by a *mountain* if the *dragon* doesn't get me first!"

"Val!" the bard snapped. "Trust me, I understand. Just *ask* me!"

"*That's* what you choose to focus on right now?"

"*Ask!*"

Val grit her teeth as more of the mountain came undone. "Help. Me. Please," she ground out.

The bard smiled grimly, the glow around her brightening, and her dark hair started floating around her face. Val saw flames dancing in the bard's eyes.

"We need to get these eggs out of here," Val told her, before the bard could charge off to do who knew what. The bard's eyes widened in wonder when she saw what Val had hidden beneath her.

It was then that a sudden quiet fell. Gooseflesh appeared on Val's skin as the deafening silence pressed on her ears. She turned toward where Shastrith and Calliah had been. Shastrith had fallen completely still, the threads tying him to his mate and eggs nowhere to be seen, and Calliah had...changed. Her blond hair had turned a deadened, lackluster white. Her sunburns had turned to smooth, nearly translucent skin. White, archaic markings trailed up her arms, neck, and face, nearly blending in with her skin unless hit by certain angles in the light, when they would appear to writhe like snakes. Her feather was gone. In its place, she held a long, bone-white blade. One edge was smooth and razor sharp, the other was as jagged as Shastrith's teeth.

Without moving her body, Calliah swiveled her head slowly to look at Val. Shastrith's head moved at the same time, perfect mirrors of each other. When they fixed their gazes on Val, she wanted to crawl out of her skin to get away from them. They had the same deadened, silver stare that spoke of a thousand horrors.

And the worst part was that Calliah looked wholly, completely sane.

The bard stepped in front of Val, her body wreathed in golden flames.

Calliah's eyes widened fractionally. "*You.*" Her hand tightened around her blade. Her blood—pure, milky white—dripped down its edge. Fire built in Shastrith's throat, hissing as he cracked open his jaw.

"What have you done, Calliah?" the bard asked, her magic growing ever larger around her.

Calliah sneered. "Calliah died the day her 'friends' and a pathetic bard betrayed her," she hissed. "Xexus, the last of Mother Night's priestesses, is my title." She snapped her fingers, and more fire hissed in Shastrith's mouth, smoke billowing from his jaws as his chest glowed red with flames. "And I believe my new friend has something he wishes to say."

The world ground to a halt for Val, her panic and fear slowing everything down and drawing it into focus. In that moment, with the eggs tucked tightly against her body, her magic flared, and she saw the threads of magic swirling around the other women. Thick, solid strands tied the bard directly to the earth, and one swept away from her heart into the far distance. Xexus' strands were more erratic. One barbed, silvery strand tied her to her new blade. The other was double stranded but frayed, like yarn coming undone, and tied her directly to Shastrith, whose core was frighteningly empty, as if his soul had vanished. Xexus had no one else. No other ties—no other loved ones.

Val felt the pull of the earth at her feet—the pull of the eggs and the people she had helped in the world at large. There was something solid and beautiful about those ties. She may have lost her mother, but there was still a place for her in this world. A place, it seemed, that Xexus had shunned.

Val focused on the tenuous bond between Xexus and Shastrith. She imagined it shattering—breaking into thousands of pieces the same way her mother's had. The thread shuddered. Neither Shastrith nor Xexus seemed to notice. All Val saw was the identical bloodlust in their eyes. They would kill anything in sight. The bard. Val. And the eggs.

Val grit her teeth. Her mother hadn't waited for the fight to come to her. And neither would Val.

She lurched away from the eggs and ran toward Xexus and Shastrith. The bard cried out for her to stop. Xexus looked on with bored pity.

Until Val grabbed hold of the thread connecting her to the dragon.

Xexus and Shastrith both convulsed, collapsing. Blinding pain wrenched through Val's gut and coursed through her spine into her mind. She grit her teeth against it even as she felt blood pouring from her nose. Whatever pact Xexus had made, Val would break it. For her mother, her kingdom, and for the dragon himself. The magic seared into Val's skin, but she grabbed it with both hands. The dragon scale bracelet flashed on her wrist.

"STOP!" Xexus howled, lunging at Val.

The snap rang like thunder through the cavern. Xexus screamed. Shastrith roared. The mountain shook. Golden warmth wrapped around Val before the pain shut off the world around her.

THERE WERE stars overhead when Val awoke. Stars and smoke.

She lurched up, expecting to see half the mountain burning from dragon fire. Her body screamed at her, but she brushed that aside as she looked frantically around. But there was no mountainside ablaze. No dragon roars. Only the smoking rubble of what had been Shastrith's cave.

"Do you know how many people I've had to drag out of falling mountains?"

Val whipped around and found the bard perched atop a pile of debris—a pile of the bard's belongings scattered at her feet. The bard had several cuts along her arms and face, but most of the blood had dried. Val couldn't tell if the dark circles beneath the bard's eyes were from soot or exhaustion.

"More than one?" Val hazarded a guess, grimacing at the aches and pains lancing through her whole body.

"*One* is too many!"

But Val hardly heard her. Her hand had brushed against a large, brittle bone protruding from beneath the cave's wreckage. Tears sprang to her eyes. "Where's Shastrith?" she asked hoarsely.

"Gone," the bard said, just as quiet and pained. "He flew off, carrying his new mistress on his back."

"So I did *nothing*." Val clenched her teeth and huddled against herself. "Why didn't you stop them?" she accused the bard.

The bard shrugged, her mouth pulled tight. "They didn't ask for my help. You did, so I had to protect you before all else." She gestured to the rubble, which Val should have been buried beneath. But instead the eggs...Oh, Sister *Earth*, the eggs.

Val scoffed to mask her trembling lip. "A lot of good I was to rescue. I'm worthless. I couldn't even save one dragon." The tears started then, thick and silent down her cheeks.

"You're right," the bard said. "You didn't save one." She drew out a large, bulging sack from behind her, huffing with exertion. She gingerly set it down and loosened the drawstring that kept it closed. "You saved five."

The dragon eggs glittered in the moonlight, nearly too big for the knapsack. But they were all safe. All still alive.

Val wept and went to them, drawing the sack close to her. "But how will they survive?" she asked the bard, as if expecting her to have the answers to everything. "They don't have any parents left to take care of them. I've only delayed the inevitable!"

"Val." The bard put her hand over Val's and looked deeply into her face, as if she could stare into her very soul. "You were a hero today. Dragons are hearty creatures, and so are their eggs. As long as they are kept safe, they will hatch when the time is right."

Val snorted, even as her limbs trembled from residual fear and grief. "Not much of a hero when all I'm doing is trying to fix my mistakes." She sighed and leaned forward, bitterness clawing at her throat as she thought of her mother's voice—of the sacrifice she had made that Val had completely undone. "I should have known magic like that was too good to be true."

"Unfortunately, all good intentions have unforeseen consequences." There was a hollowness to the bard's voice that carried lifetimes of sorrow. She squeezed Val's hand and tapped the dragon scale bracelet on her wrist. "Your mother knew that, too. You carry her mantle well." She gestured to the eggs.

More tears spilled down Val's face as she looked at the eggs. As she watched them, tendrils of magic—soft, tentative threads—trailed from her chest and connected to each egg in turn. Warmth and comfort bloomed inside her. She trailed her thumb over their smooth, jewel-toned shells and absently hummed her mother's lullaby to them, her throat tight with emotion.

"You have delayed a great evil today by severing that connection between Xexus and Shastrith," the bard said, her face soft but somehow regal. "It will take them decades to rebuild it, which gives future generations more time to prepare." She tilted her head. "If you could receive any reward for your heroism, what would it be?"

Val let out a bark of incredulous laughter. "I don't suppose you have a place I can stay and protect some dragon eggs, do you?"

The bard grinned, her eyes flashing gold. "I think you'd be surprised what I can do. All you have to do is ask."

DEMON'S PACT

Hate seeks hate
And in hate she found him
Alone
Bitter
Betrayed
Only tethered to life
By the chains of vengeance.

Hate knows hate
And he saw hate in her
Alone
Bitter
Betrayed
"What is it you seek
From the last of the dragons?"

"I seek what is mine
I seek what was taken."
Rage

Longing
Sorrow
"What you wish for I cannot give.
One cannot steal what is Death's."

He knew this truth all too well
Caged within his cave of memories.
Rage
Longing
Sorrow
He suffered it all
As he battered against his fate.

"I aim to rectify the phoenix' mistake
Your power can aid me like none other can."
Cunning
Desperation
Hope
"Laws written by imperfect gods
Must wallow in imperfection by nature."

He considered her
Silver eyes burned with light.
Cunning
Desperation
Hope
Could this small daughter of Man
Free him where his own power could not?

"What will I receive
In exchange for my power?"
"New life."
"I have lived too many."
"Dominion over all Man."

"What use have I for Man?"
"Vengeance upon your foes."
"Death has embraced them long ago."
"Save for one.
The last phoenix lives on."

The dragon stopped in shuddering breath.
So Death had played his favorites?
Rage
Fury
Betrayal
The dragon sold his soul that day
To claim his morsel of justice.

She consumed his sacrifice
Her own justice trailing flames.
Abandoned
Forgotten
Betrayed
Xexus, the demoness born
Refused to bow to Laws for ever more.

SWORD OF WHISPERS

Sword of feather
Sword of bone
Cursed be thy wielder
Lest thy wielder be they born

Sword of darkness
Sword of love
The lives you reap
Be the lives you keep

Sword of Mother
Sword of Daughter
The Ancient Laws you tear apart
To bring back life from whence it starts.

Sword of curses
Sword of pain
Lost to prisoners' ruins
By prisoner's pow'r

Sword of shadow
Sword of mist
The servant searches
With madness as friend

Sword of power
Sword of night
To your mistress one day you'll return
And together the world will burn

WHERE DEMONS REST

Twenty-five years after the battle of Giant's Quell, a plague swept across the slowly mending pieces of Loralan. Doctors and historians alike have theorized this sickness to be an aggressive, widespread form of cancer that was no respecter of age, race, or gender. However, so many bodies were burned or improperly preserved that further research has so far been thwarted.

Agricultural villages were especially affected by this plague, shaking the foundations of the kingdom's infrastructure. It decimated hundreds in a matter of months, both to sickness and starvation, and showed little signs of abating as the years dragged on. Final mortality estimations count anywhere from 140,000 people to nearly 1.2 million. Again, due to hasty burial processes, these numbers are left to speculation.

With his kingdom on the verge of ruin, King Varkrim II sent any men still breathing to chase down rumors that had been whispered through shadowed corridors and mourner's lips. A treasure abandoned in the ruins of the great T'elemeth fortress, said to grant any wish. A demon sword awaiting a new master.

-J. Lashton; *By Her People: A History of Loralan's Common Folk (265th edition)*; pg. 437

" I don't *care* about a stupid wish!"

"Brin," Traz leaned heavily on his crutch while he rubbed his brow, his stump of a leg throbbing almost as much as his head. He hoisted his knapsack higher on his shoulder and faced his eight-year-old brother, whose eyes were bright and stubborn beneath the filth on his face. "I already told you. I *have* to go. King's orders."

Brin folded his arms—his thread-bare, too small rags pulling tight against his little body—and jutted his chin out. "But he said anyone that *can*." Brin stared pointedly at Traz's leg. Or lack thereof.

Traz's jaw tightened. Pain crawled up his thigh. Brin was right. According to anyone that had a voice for opinion, Traz didn't *have* to go. He'd heard it more times than he could count. But as he took in the sagging roof overhead, cracked walls, beds that were nothing more than rags, and meager food-stores that had been ravaged by starving vermin, Traz's duty was clear. The only one with money left to give in this goddess-forsaken village was the king. "Think how much money we could get. We could get you shoes, and a new bed, and as many apples as you want. Wouldn't that make you happy?"

"I *am* happy, see?" Brin bared his teeth in a terrifying, forced mockery of a smile. His stomach grumbled, and he wrapped his arms around it, ears pink. "See? Even my stomach says so! So now you don't have to go!"

Traz glanced out the entry of their little hut, where the door hung from loose hinges and shot slivers at any that dared touch it. The rest of the village men were almost done with gathering their equipment and saying goodbye to their families. They'd be leaving soon, and no matter how many bribes and favors Traz had paid them, they would leave without him if he weren't ready in time. He had to get going. *Now*. He didn't have time for another power struggle. "Brin, I have to go. Mathilde said she'd keep an eye on you, but you have to feed yourself, and—"

Brin collided with him, bony shoulders clacking against bony hips, hands wrapped tight about Traz's waist. "*NO!*"

Some of the other men glanced over in annoyance, boring holes of pity into Traz's face. Jaw set so tight his teeth almost cracked, Traz ushered Brin deeper inside their hut and slammed the door behind them. He cursed at the new slivers in his hand. "What is *wrong* with you?" he asked Brin.

"Don't go, Traz! Please don't go!" Brin buried his face in Traz's tunic, soaking it with his tears. "What if you don't come back?"

Traz froze, his heart fracturing in his chest. Although Brin hadn't said it, Traz knew why he was so afraid. They had both watched that day, early in the plague, when the village healers herded their parents to the quarantine huts at the edge of the village. The healers had shoved Brin and Traz back into the home their father had built and told them to fend for themselves until their parents returned. Before anyone knew what the sickness was. Before they knew there was no way to predict its spread, and that there was no cure. It had been the last time Traz and Brin saw their parents before a rickety cart had rolled them to a mass grave.

Traz's leg ached again, reaching fingers of pain up through his body. That same sickness had already taken his leg. Had taken their livelihood, and had made them watch as whatever meager comforts they had left withered around them. Traz would walk to the Pit and back before he let the sickness rob Brin of anything else.

He eased himself down to Brin's level, wobbling against his crutch for balance, and made his brother look at him. "I'm going to come back."

Brin rubbed his nose on the back of his sleeve. "Nobody's come back from trying to find that sword. Robest told me so! He says a demon kills everyone that tries!"

Traz pursed his lips. Curse that ten-year-old blabber-mouth. Robest would grow up to be just as much a gossip as his father, the tavern owner, if he kept this up. "So far, that's been true—"

"It killed all those soldiers! And freed a dragon!"

"You're not wrong, but—"

"Robest said the demon helped *another* demon escape, too! What if there are *two* of them there?"

"No one's said anything about two—"

"But how would *you* know? Everyone that's gone there is dead!"

Traz rubbed his face. "Fair," he said trying to ward off the anxiety radiating from Brin. These were things he had considered himself but had tried to ignore. It didn't matter, really. Traz's fear and worry and inner cowardice didn't matter. Doing nothing was a sure way to get him killed. At least going to find the sword offered a *chance* of success, slim as it might be. Even when failure could lead to a horrific end.

"Don't go, Traz! Don't let a demon eat you!"

"Brin!" Traz smooshed Brin's cheeks between his palms in desperation and made him look up at him. "I'm not going to die! I... I have a secret."

Brin wrenched his face away and rubbed his tears from his cheeks. "You do?" he asked, looking skeptical. "What is it?"

Traz cast about for a suitable lie to back up his paltry claim. "I'm not after the wish."

"You're not? Then why—"

"I'm going to get the sword for the king, and that's it. Everyone else is going to get their own wishes, but not me. I'll be pure of heart, and that's how I'll win."

"That doesn't make—a-any sense." Brin's cries had turned to breathless hiccups, but at least the tears had stopped. He gave Traz a dubious look. "It sounds stupid."

Traz sighed, deflated, and sat on the dusty floor. "It does, doesn't it?" He held his arms open, and Brin snuggled close to him. Traz wrapped his arms around him and rested his chin on his head. "All right, so I lied. I don't have a secret way to get the sword."

"Good, 'cause it was dumb anyway."

"But I *do* promise I'll come home. I'm not going to die. I've already survived the sickness once," he gestured to his stump leg. "You think I'll let a make-believe demon get me after something like that?"

"It's *not* make believe! And Robest said *everyone* dies, no matter what!"

Traz pulled a face at him. "And who are you going to believe? A skinny bully, or your big brother that's never let you down before?"

That elicited a ghost of a smile. "You, I guess," Brin said in a small voice, eyes magnified behind his residual tears. "But only if you don't come up with anymore stupid plans."

Traz flicked Brin's nose with a smile. "Deal. Now let's go before I get left behind."

Brin helped him up, and together they walked to the village square.

There was not a dry eye in the crowd of women, children, and elderly that had gathered around the expedition party in the main square. No one tried to hide it. Despair had become a daily habit over the past few years. However, the expedition party stood proud and tight-lipped, trying to portray nothing but confidence for their families. They did a poor job at it, though. Their eyes were too wide, their jaws and fists too tight, and their knees locked so rigidly they threatened to buckle. None of them were heroes. Just men with no options left.

Dravek, the village elder's son—large and sturdy as an oak tree—stood at the front of the crowd. Next to Dravek was a lithe man wrapped in a stark white cloak emblazoned with King Varkrim II's scarlet emblem; a courier, too clean and pressed and soft-skinned to belong in a place like Belkit village. To have suffered the way they all had. Most everyone avoided him, casting glances of distaste and distrust over their shoulders. They may have been subject to the king, but their days of reverence had long since passed.

Dravek raised his hands as the sun hit the peak of the nearest hut, watery in the gray dawn. "Men of Belkit," he said, "I'm sorry, but the time has come." He twisted a woven wedding band around his finger. "The sickness has made us too accustomed to goodbyes, but has yet to make them easier. I know that as well as all of you." He straightened his shoulders, and looked each of them in the eye. "But perhaps this endeavor can put an end to farewells that come too soon. Leave your parting wishes, and a rousing cheer for the heroes we are soon to become."

A meager round of support fell limp among the men. Tears continued to course down their families' faces. Traz took in their motley crew, and himself, with a grimace. Skinny, starving farmers and tanners and tavern-owners. Plow boys and shepherds. Not one of them a warrior. Pathetic 'heroes', the lot of them. He hugged Brin close to his side.

Dravek gave them a tight smile and motioned to the courier. "This is Samuel. He brings a message from the king."

Samuel stepped forward, his cloak flapping about him with nary a thread out of place. He looked across the crowd not with the cold indifference Traz had anticipated, but something softer. Kinder. "Greetings from King Varkrim II to the village of Belkit. He has sent me to bid you thanks for your noble service in assisting him in the recovery of the demon queen's sword."

Brin tugged on Traz's sleeve. "How'd it get lost?"

"Robest didn't tell you that?" Traz asked with no small amount of petty victory.

Brin stuck his tongue out at him. "Just tell me."

"Another demon freed the queen from a fortress thirty years ago. They say he lost the sword while fighting the guards."

"Not a very good demon, is he?"

"Must not be."

Samuel motioned to a cart full of sacks. "You will find provisions of ale and the finest warrior's fare the kingdom can offer."

An audible gasp sounded from the villagers. Traz's stomach grumbled. *Food.* Real food. Not rations tainted by grubs and time. Traz had no idea what was in those sacks, but his mouth already salivated at the thought.

"Do you think there are any apples in there?" Brin asked, mouth dangling open as he looked at the sacks.

"I wouldn't doubt it," Traz said.

"*Lucky.*"

"The rations you will receive now for your journey," Samuel said. "You will receive your gold payment after the sword is recovered."

A man just downwind of Traz leaned to his neighbor. "Be nice if we got paid now so we could give it to our families in case we—" he cut his words off before he could finish the thought. His wife's hand had clamped on his arm like a claw.

"A meal is payment enough," she said through clenched teeth. "Though it is certainly the *least* Varkrim could do for us."

"I promise, your provisions will be divvied out in but a moment," Samuel said over the murmurs and rumblings. "I must finish my message, and then the rest is to do with as you see fit."

The crowd grew quiet again, and Samuel nodded his thanks. "King Varkrim has dispatched ten other villages on this same mission," he said. "When you reach T'elemeth, King Varkrim urges you to spend the night with your groups and not search the ruins until morning. That is when it will be safest."

"And how does our *esteemed* king know this?" An older woman stepped through the crowd, gray hair in tatters and back stooped with grief. Traz remembered her from days when she would swap recipes with his mother. Graim was her name. She'd had nine sons. The sickness had taken seven, and now her last two were in the group ready to depart. The life had left her a long time ago, clouding her eyes and making her bones brittle with bitterness. Traz couldn't blame her. "How many villages have you sent to their ruin before ours?"

Samuel tightened his jaw, his eyes soft with empathy. "I'm afraid I am only here to relay the King's messages. I cannot answer for him."

"I bet you *are* afraid, holed up in your palaces eating meats and pastries while the rest of us die for the kingdom that can't protect us." She raised her head as high as her stooped back would allow, all the lines in her face pulled taut with anger. "How many of us died in the Giant's Quell? You don't hear about the hundreds of common people sent to slay the demon queen's dragon with nothing but rakes and saws for weapons. We were naught but fodder, but we did our duty. We fought our fight and were trampled beneath that black dragon's claws. We bled him to his last drops." She straightened, lips pressed tight. "But who are the heroes? The knights bedecked in glittering armor that wrapped chains around him as they waded through *our* blood."

Graim's sons wound through the crowd to get to her, trying to quiet her as they tossed alarmed glances at Samuel, but Graim waved them away. "And even after all that, you couldn't keep that dragon and his mistress locked away properly! T'elemeth fell because of this kingdom's stupidity. All that death for *nothing*!" A ragged, phlegmy cough ripped through her words and body, rattling in her lungs. Traz had heard that sound before. The sound of death clawing at a sickness sufferer's throat.

Graim hunched over to curb the fit, but looked at the courier with blazing eyes. "Why should we give the wish to a kingdom that despises us, when we could use it to build our own?"

Silence settled like a shroud over the crowd as all eyes turned to Samuel. He watched them, face agonized. Moisture filled his eyes, and his spine seemed near collapse. He opened his mouth, words hovering at the corners of his mouth. But then he slammed it shut, stiffened his shoulders, and looked away from Graim. "King Varkrim urges you to—to make merry when you reach the ruins. He thanks you for your service to the kingdom. But... But I—" His voice broke, and he turned his back on the crowd. "I would not condemn you for using that sword as you see fit."

No one said anything; couldn't form the words.

Dravek moved to redirect the crowd, but another man beat him to it. Troth, an overindulgent regular at the local tavern. "Let us dwell on that sword when we get it. Best not let these supplies go to waste! Let's go, men!" He threw them each a pack. A few hit men in the face in their daze. Traz nearly toppled over from the weight of it, but Brin caught him.

Dravek took control and called them into formation. The men snuck the food supplies to their families before forming haphazard lines. Traz handed his entire pack to Brin. "This will be too heavy for me. Take it."

Brin's smile nearly split his face at the red, shining apples nestled at the top of the bag. He handed the biggest one to Traz. "You have to eat, too."

Traz smiled and tucked it into a pocket, blinking back tears. He hugged Brin and kissed him on the top of his dirty hair. "Be good for Mathilde. I'll be back before you know it."

Brin melted into him. "I love you, Traz."

"I love you too," Traz said. He choked back the emotion that threatened in his throat.

Brin stood back and puffed out his chest, trying to stop his quivering lip. "Go be a hero. I'll keep the house safe while you're gone."

Traz smiled, his eyes misty. "I know you will, buddy," he said. He ruffled Brin's hair and limped into formation.

When they were all organized, they waved a final goodbye to their families and marched away from the village. Their procession started small. Quiet. Only punctuated by the sound of their footsteps, ragged breaths, and a few tears. Most had never left the village, especially not since the sickness had broken out. A swell of anxiety washed over Traz. What was he doing? What were *any* of them doing? This wasn't just stepping out to find food or search for more healers. This was *magic.* Magic and fairy tales and wars and dragons beyond anything he had ever known. But he couldn't stop now. *Wouldn't* stop. He pushed aside his terror and continued his march.

The moment they took their first stop to rest, Troth broke out a store of ale. "We may have given away our food spoils, but this is *ours* to enjoy. Drink up while you can, lads!"

Everyone glanced to Dravek, and he nodded once. They all dug into their bags and withdrew the amber bottles. As the alcohol flowed, tensions released from the men's shoulders and hearts. Songs and crude jokes spilled from their lips in broken syllables, and even as they began their march again, their revelries did not stop until they reached T'elemeth two days later.

As the sinking sun dyed the clouds scarlet, the group crested a hill and took their first look at T'elemeth. A shudder ran down Traz's spine. The stories told around the village—terrifying as they might be—had not done the place justice. A sort of presence hung about the valley below, heavy and dank and draped across the skeletal, blackened trees like a funeral shroud. The burnt forest stretched the entirety of the valley, save for the center where the scorched, crumbling ruins of a fortress huddled around a great, yawning pit like broken ribs. A pit meant for a dragon.

"One dragon did all this?" Traz asked himself.

"Scared?" Troth asked, cheeks pink with alcohol. "I'd tell you to go home, but I don't think you'd survive the journey."

Traz's face paled with anger, but he couldn't say anything, especially not when he feared the same thing. He curled his knuckles tighter around his crutch. No. He *would* make it back, however he could.

"Standing and staring won't do us any good," Dravek said, already making his way down the hill. He motioned the others to follow him. "Come on. We have a wish to find."

"Are we sure we have to take it to the king?" Troth asked. "I've got some wishes I'd like to make. Ones with lots of gold."

"You'll only get to wish after *I* do, Troth," someone else chimed in. "I'll wish to be the richest king in the world. You can have whatever money's left over."

The other men joined in.

"I'd wish to live forever! No more worrying about the sickness for me!"

"I'd wish for land that grows spices and sweet meat all year round!"

"I'd wish for the most beautiful wife in the world."

Traz ground his teeth. Drunken idiots, all of them. What if the sword only had one wish to give? Or maybe two? They'd waste all the magic before they had a chance to do any good with it. Traz couldn't risk it. He had one wish, and one wish only. And he'd fight off anyone he had to to get it. Looking at all the faces, though, beaming with alcohol-laced enthusiasm, he saw a danger lurking in their too-bright eyes. The sickness had cast misery in a wide-net across the kingdom, and these men were willing to shed blood for any small happiness they could muster. Traz would have to be careful. A demon would not be the only danger in T'elemeth tonight.

As they approached the treeline, a shabby figure came into view. A dusty bard waited for them at the edge of the black forest, bedecked in bright, ill-fitting greens and yellows. He had a face that was neither old nor young, probably a performer's trick. No hair, but scarlet tattoos and symbols curled their way across his bald scalp, cheekbones, nose, and jaw. They undulated in the fading light like charmed serpents waiting to strike. Traz supposed the bard had painted them for dramatic flair. The man's eyes caught his attention more than the painted lines, though. Thick, dark eyebrows hooded small, milky eyes that darted sightlessly from one sound to the next. He was blind.

He smiled at the group's approach. "You are the first to arrive," he said. "What village do you hail from?"

"Belkit," Dravek said, crossing his arms. Traz saw him wrap his fingers around the hunting knife he kept sheathed around his ribs. "Who might you be? And how did you know we were coming?"

"Ambrose is the name," the bard said. "I have been watching villages come in waves for many months, now. I thought I might offer my services to ones so brave."

"We have little money."

"A single coin and drop of ale is all I need for my time."

The group's tension eased as Ambrose and Dravek chatted. A blind bard could do them little harm. Traz leaned on his crutch, fighting the ache in his foot and up his leg. New blisters had formed on his hand and the ball of his foot, and he wasn't sure if his boot sole would survive the journey back. He munched on the apple Brin had given him. The sweet gush of juice shocked his mouth and almost elicited a smile. Brin. This was all for Brin. Soon he would have all the apples in the world he could want.

Ambrose had seemed to come to an agreement with Dravek. He stood, brushing filth from his costume and casting his unseeing eyes across the group. "If you'd like to follow me, I can show you to your campsite."

Dravek raised an eyebrow. "You know the way?"

"Why should we follow a blind old man like you?" Troth asked, making a face.

The bard smiled serenely, never showing his teeth. "You'd be surprised how long I've been here, and what I've seen with these blind eyes." Something about the words chilled Traz's blood.

Ambrose waved them on, and, with no other ideas on how to proceed, they followed, passing beneath the scorched trees with a quiet, terrified reverence. Those still drunk grew sober quickly. There was no sound—their footsteps muffled by ash—except for the tinkling of bells. Traz looked for them until he saw them draped across the fractured canopy. They were *everywhere*, strung together across every tree-limb they could reach, their silver stark against the rotting wood.

"What do you think they're for?" one man asked barely above a whisper.

The man next to him shrugged. "It's magic. How am I supposed to know?"

"They're meant to ward off demons," Ambrose said. Traz couldn't believe the bard had heard the remark so well. "They also mask the sound of the demon sword."

"Sound?" Traz asked before he could stop himself.

"The sword wails whenever there is death nearby. The more death, the louder it screams." Ambrose looked back, eyes darting back and forth. It almost seemed as if he could see *through* Traz. "Some say the demon created the sickness just to lure more people to their deaths, so that it can use the sword's own call to find it."

Dravek cuffed the back of the bard's head. "Enough. We have enough ghosts without you filling our heads with more."

No one said anything else. The hairs on the back of Traz's neck stood on end. Could it be true? Was this all just a ruse to lead them to their deaths? The feeling of eyes watching him prickled up his spine.

His heart pounded against his chest. *Run, run, run!* But they kept moving; deeper into the forest that seemed intent to swallow them whole. What other choice did they have? They would get the sword, and its wish. *Traz* would. No one breathed a word, save for the bard, who hummed to himself.

When they finally exited the tree-line, they each breathed a collective sigh of relief, as if anvils had been lifted from their shoulders. They settled around and set up a fire, each too nervous to be caught in the ruins alone after dark. As they sat, more groups arrived through the forest from every direction. The village groups nodded to each other uneasily, but otherwise kept to themselves. Ambrose bowed away from the group to wish the others welcome. More fires sprouted in the dark. Clouds rolled over the sky and blotted out the stars and moon, and as the rest of the world grew quiet, the ale began to flow and the music began.

> *Dark in the deeps of T'elemeth*
> *Lies a sword 'twixt life and death.*
> *A wish it grants to those who ask*
> *But 'tis no easy task*
> *A demon waits to steal it back*
> *And claim your final breath*

Sparks fizzed into the starless, overcast night as men roared the notes, their cheeks red from the bonfires's heat. Ale overflowed their mugs, dripping glittering amber drops into the hissing flames. Laughter erupted. Bodies staggered between each other, patting backs and clanging mugs. Traz tucked his leg as far beneath him as he could to keep from getting tripped over.

Idiots, he thought to himself. *We couldn't have made ourselves anymore obvious to a demon.*

> *Yonder to ruins*
> *Forward to fate*

Ride ye, oh brave ones
Past demon's death.
Onward to victr'y
Your truest wish to make

The other campfires scattered about the dark plains sputtered like fireflies. The uncertain light shared glimpses of the eager, anxious faces gathered around them. Ambrose stood at one of them, swaying and singing as he played his mandolin. Traz's heart sunk at the sight. In their drunken stupor, it had all become a game to them; a festival of bravery and strength and magic. For a moment, they had forgotten about the wish, and he had a feeling that lapse would cost them dearly.

"To the ruins of T'elemeth!" Troth raised his mug to the looming tower behind them, eying the crowd. "To the treasure she holds just for us!" A round of cheers erupted around him.

Traz scoffed. *Us?* No such thing. He knew enough about greed and power to know that the moment the sword was found, all friendships and bonds of any kind would crumble as completely as the ruins behind them. He had to be the one to find it first. Even if he had to tear the hillside down to its blackened roots.

"What makes us think we can find it?" Another man swayed precariously from his generous helpings of ale and blinked at Troth with bleary concern. "A demon lost it thirty years ago. A *demon*. If he can't find it, then why can we?"

The camp quieted, casting uneasy glances the man's way. Though they may have felt the same, their drink hadn't loosened their tongues as readily. No one liked the doom sucking the warmth from their alcohol-laden blood.

"Countless men have died on this very plain from those thoughts." Dravek rose to his feet, the words a deep growl in his chest. He nearly drowned out the firelight with his massive frame. "So many hundreds have run themselves through on the gentle sword of doubt." He swept his gaze across the gathered men. None could meet him in the eye. "If you continue those thoughts, you will find no better fate than they. Swallowed up in the demon's maw." A somber, dreadful hush settled over them at the thought. Dravek left them in silence for five counts before he spread his arms wide. "Each one of you has lost someone, either to the kingdom or to the plague. I intend to find that sword. Get my wish. Return home a hero. Whatever the cost. And I know you intend the same."

A half-hearted cheer of agreement grew into a fervent roar of brazen bravado as the men realized what he had said. The wish no longer belonged to the kingdom. It belonged to whoever could find it first. Another roar. Another collective draft of ale. Traz refrained.

"Not *everyone* can be a hero, can they?" Troth sneered in Traz's ear when Dravek wandered back into the crowd. "Little cripple got to slow us down the entire way, didn't he? And for what? To watch the rest of us find the sword before you can crest the hill?" He poured a trickle of ale over Traz's head. "What *is* your wish, little leach? Hoping to keep your little brother from abandoning your sorry self?"

Traz turned toward the man, jaw clenched. The ale sunk deep in his hair, burning his scalp. "Leave Brin out of this, Troth."

Troth blinked owlishly at him through red-rimmed eyes. He cracked a grin, his alcohol laden breath nearly suffocating Traz. "Y'know, I think I figured it out. I know why you came. You'd be the perfect demon bait! Useful to everyone! It'll take that monster at least a few minutes to gnaw through that wooden leg of yours." He tapped Traz's crutch with his boot, his cackle filling his lungs with flem until he choked. "Thanks for your sacrifice. You're a genuine hero!"

Anger flared in Traz's cheeks, but he couldn't—*wouldn't*—retaliate. He collected his crutch and hobbled away.

"Better get your runnin' practice in!" Troth said. "Won't do you any good!"

Traz's hand clenched around his crutch and he tightened his jaw until his teeth ached. He had to stay invisible. They would forget about him in the sword-finding frenzy. He could wait it out and then find the sword in peace.

Or he could search for it now.

The thought raced through him and curdled his stomach. Maybe he could find the sword before any bloodshed had to happen at all. But, as he looked at the looming, silent walls, dread prickled his ears and made them ring. Every whisper of breeze was the rustle of a demon lurking in the brush. Every dark, impenetrable corner a hiding place for death. Traz's mouth ran dry, and he kept walking. He didn't know how far he dared go, but he had to at least try.

Traz stubbed his foot on a protruding piece of wall. The jolt frightened him more than hurt. He dropped to the ground with a curse, heart hammering in his ribs. His crutch clattered beside him, and he nursed the injured toe. "Rotting pile of rubbish!" He kicked over the offending debris.

"I couldn't agree more."

Traz jumped violently and smacked his head against the wall behind him. Dazed, he tried to get up and run, but forgot he was missing a critical appendage. He fumbled his crutch, tripped forward, and crashed into another wall. It collapsed beneath him, and dust plumed around him. *I'm going to die here! Brin, I'm sorry!*

No. No, no, *NO!* He had promised. Not even the Pit would keep him from getting back home.

Strong arms grabbed him by the shoulders and wrenched him from the wreckage.

"Hands off, demon!" Traz shouted, his voice cracking. He swung and missed. He scrabbled around for something, *anything,* to use as a weapon. This was *not* how he died.

"I'm no demon, boy," a voice said, mild but firm. "But I could understand the confusion."

The dust settled, and Traz's heart stopped. The thing was the most horrible, disfigured attempt at human form he'd seen. It wore tattered clothing, and a scabbard strapped around its waist. Burn scars bubbled over its eyes, nose, and cheeks, the skin puckered and blotched with angry red marks. It had no eyebrows and a gaping hole in the right side of its head where an ear should have been. White tufts of hair poked out from the few unburned spots on its scalp. Its eyes were the only things untouched. Gray, clear, and calculating.

Traz finally wrapped his fingers around his crutch.

He swung again, full force. Crutch whistling through the air. No questions. No hesitation. Just pure panicked instinct. Adrenaline flooded his ears and rushed blood to his face.

The demon caught the crutch before it made contact and watched Traz with a crooked smile. "What was that for?"

Traz's heart pummeled his chest, his eyes bugging with adrenaline even as the blood fled from his face. "What do you want from me?"

"Easy, boy. I'm no monster. I won't eat you. I just want you to leave." It relinquished its hold on Traz's crutch and sat next to him, arms and legs splayed as if it were on a picnic. It tucked the sword behind it, and chuckled at Traz's scandalized face. Traz scooted a few inches away. It didn't seem to notice, but took in the view of the ruins and surrounding fire-blackened forest beneath the patches of moonlight that forced their way through the clouds. "You here for the treasure?"

Traz said nothing.

The demon raised an eyebrow—or at least the part of his face where an eyebrow *should* have been. "Well," it pointedly directed its gaze to Traz's lack of a leg. "You're certainly the strangest treasure hunter I've ever seen."

Traz bristled. "Have you seen *yourself* lately?" He couldn't help it. The words tumbled out, all the resentment toward the other men that thought he didn't belong fueling each syllable. How dare this *creature* doubt him, too? But as soon as the words were out, he knew it was over. No demon would ever let an insult like that slide.

But it just laughed. Long and loud. "Can't say I have, but I'll take your word for it!"

Traz watched closely for any indication of an attack. A hand to the weapon at its side. Magic forming. Would Traz even know what magic looked like, though? When nothing happened, Traz eased into a sitting position. Maybe... Maybe this was just a man after all.

The man scratched his scalp, small flakes snowing onto his shoulders. "How old are you, boy?"

Traz furrowed his brow. He still didn't trust the man, but that seemed a harmless question. "Eighteen. Why?"

The man ignored the question. "You have anyone special waiting for you at home?"

Traz pressed his lips together. Absolutely not. Brin would stay out of this. "Maybe."

"I told you I won't eat you."

"Because *that* doesn't sound suspicious at all!"

The man laughed again. "You remind me of my brother. He didn't trust anyone. It kept him alive for a long time." His eyes got a faraway look in them, and he dropped his gaze to his hands. "At least it should have." He shook his head and looked back at Traz. "You strike me as a brotherly type. You must have a brother or two at home. Is that it?"

Traz balked, mouth wide-open. How had he picked up on that so quickly? Traz tried to recover his shock, but it was too late. His reaction had been as good as any other answer.

"No parents?" the man asked, not unkindly.

Traz scowled. "No parents. Got taken by the sickness. But you probably already know that, since you're so smart."

A shadow passed over the man's face. "I'm sorry." The shadow receded, and he picked at his teeth and flicked away whatever he found. He didn't look at Traz. "That why you're out here, then? To die for your little brother's sake?"

Traz swelled with anger. Troth. Dravek. Now even a perfect stranger. None of them had any faith in him. He could stay quiet to the others' abuse, but this was too much. "I won't die. And you better watch your tongue with me, old man, before I bite it out."

"Oh hoh, we've got ourselves a scrapper, do we?" He glanced at

Traz with an expression he couldn't read. "And how does this scrapper intend to fight an *actual* demon? I'll warn you, a crutch will just make it laugh."

Traz wanted so *desperately* to throw back something substantial, to make *himself* feel better, if nothing else, but he couldn't. It wasn't an underestimation when it was true. The fury died within him. He deflated with grit teeth and turned away.

The man sighed, a tired but regretful sound. "Been awhile since I've had company. I forget how to keep it." He looked at Traz. "You got a name?"

Traz scuffed dirt with his heal. "Does it matter?"

"Wouldn't ask if it didn't matter."

Traz rolled his eyes, already tired of this game. "I've only got one if you do."

"Nelson."

Traz blinked. He hadn't expected him to answer so quickly. "I'm Traz."

Nelson looked at him with a furrowed forehead and a curled lip. "What kind of name is Traz?"

Traz gaped at him. Not even his *name* was safe from scorn? "Same kind of name as Nelson!"

The man chuckled again, a sound that infuriated Traz even more. "You've got me there, I guess." A full-body shudder made him twitch. He muttered something under his breath with a scowl and drew a small bell from his trousers, absently rolling it between his scarred hands.

Traz's stomach dropped to his toes. "Are—are you the one that strung all those bells in the trees?"

Nelson stopped and clenched the bell in his left hand, where he was missing a pinky and ring finger. "Maybe."

Traz's mouth went dry again. Unease dripped across his shoulders. "Is it true that you hung them to...to hide the sound the sword makes?"

"Among other things." He stashed the bell back in his pocket and didn't give Traz a chance to ask any more questions. "You got a wish for the treasure?"

Traz massaged his missing leg. This conversation had already exhausted him, and he was ready for it to be over. Nelson could keep his crazy. And his bells. Uproarious laughter broke through the night from a camp. "Why should I tell you? You're out here for a wish, too, and only one of them's getting granted."

"No need to worry about me. I'm not going anywhere near that thing."

Nelson's voice was low, almost too quiet for the venom he injected into the words. An involuntary shiver ran down Traz's spine. Nelson had that experience in his voice; the sound of being ripped from something he couldn't replace. The same sound Traz had when his parents died; when the healer told him...he rubbed his stump.

Nelson gave him a piercing look, as if he sensed Traz understood him. "Do you know how the sword came to T'elemeth?"

"Of course. Everyone does."

Nelson pursed his lips as if that answer wasn't good enough. "They all say that, and yet they still choose to come back here." He met Traz's eyes, his face set in grim lines. "Let me make sure you understand the price of your treasure." He stood and motioned for Traz to follow him.

Traz contemplated refusing to go. But something about Nelson's voice, and the way those unnerving gray eyes looked at him, indicated he didn't have much of a choice. He struggled to rise, situating his crutch and one good leg beneath him. A shaft of pain shot through him, and he wobbled, fighting back panic. The healer had warned him the sickness would get worse over time. The aches and pains had been coming more frequently. Traz had just hoped it wouldn't have been at such an inopportune time.

Nelson was patient as Traz got himself under control. Traz couldn't decide to be grateful or irritated.

When Traz was finally ready to move, Nelson set out toward the dungeon pit, slowing his pace just enough for Traz to follow comfortably. He zig-zagged erratically through the ruins, eyes never leaving the ground. Traz withheld a grimace and ignored the pattern. How much more of this man's insanity could he—

His boot caught something. Bells shrieked, and pain erupted in his bones. A blinding light flashed in his eyes, and then he was on the ground, gasping for breath as residual flashes blazed through his eyes.

Nelson leaned over him, the moon's light highlighting the crazed tufts of hair along his scalp. "What, did you think I do that dance just because?" He helped Traz up and got him situated with his crutch. Once the shock had worn off and he had sucked in enough oxygen to be coherent, Traz saw the strings of silver bells laid carefully across the ground and stuffed into every crevice.

"Are those...*traps*?" he asked.

"I would hope so," Nelson went on his winding path again, muttering odd things to himself while he rested his hand on the sword at his side. "Just be grateful you aren't a demon. They're much worse for him."

"Don't see how they could be." Traz made sure to follow Nelson's footsteps exactly, no matter how crazy he knew he looked.

They walked that way for several more minutes until they reached the center of the ruins; the dragon pit. Traz kept a dubious eye on the massive, seemingly unending void as they neared it. The camps had stayed far from it for good reason. Updrafts billowed from the depths of the earth; breath from the abyss. They circulated a miasma of foul stench that Traz recognized all too well: the smell of death. Black, slimy moss crawled its way through the opening, and when Nelson stepped on it, it peeled away with his boot like rotting corpse skin. Traz kept his distance.

Nelson leaned out over the pit, perilously close to falling headlong into it. "I was here when they brought the demon queen and her beast." He fell silent, his eyes glazed as he toyed with the carrion moss. "It was a colossal, black dragon spewing flames as searing as the depths of the Devil's Pit. His mistress was a tiny thing—looked only a few years older than you—but her power was darker than his hide." Traz could almost sense the memories playing behind Nelson's eyes.

Traz waited in the eerie stillness for Nelson to continue. He didn't. He had lost him. Traz should have left then. *Wanted* to leave. *No one* had survived the attack on T'elemeth. Nelson was delusional, and a waste of his time. But, despite himself, curiosity burst from his mouth unbidden. "Oh yeah? Then can you tell me how they got free?"

Nelson blinked and pulled absently at one of his tufts of hair. "One of her servants came to save her."

Traz furrowed his brow. He hadn't expected a response, much less one so matter-of-fact. "If a *demoness* couldn't get herself out, how would a servant do her any good?"

Nelson crouched at the lip of the crater and pulled his bell out again. He held it loosely in one hand and let it run across his fingers, one at a time, back and forth. "You know the Ancient Laws. Magic bound is magic beaten. She couldn't do anything for herself in chains, but if someone loosed her bonds, that would be it." Nelson shrugged. "I don't pretend to understand how it works. That's just what the books say." He let out a shuddering breath. "The servant convinced T'elemeth's sorcerer that he was a monk aiming to bless the prison to keep the demoness' powers at bay. The fool prison sorcerer let him in." Nelson met Traz's eyes, the moonlight casting strange, silvery shadows across his uneven scars. The hairs on the back of Traz's neck stand on end. Groups of men filled the empty corpse of the prison grounds, but he and Nelson felt alone in the world. The night had grown unnaturally still.

"It all…happened so fast. One moment, he was with us, the next moment, the prison doors flung open and *she* was there. Terrible and beautiful all at once."

Traz leaned forward, heart in his throat. Something about the way Nelson spoke—the wistful, haunted look in his eyes—made him start to believe that Nelson wasn't as crazy a he appeared. These were not stories of a deranged mind. These were *memories*, real and tangible and horrifying. Traz couldn't tear himself away.

"We almost had them." Nelson's voice was far away, a haunted expression on his face. "But that witch she...she turned her sword on her servant. She ran him through without a second thought. I've never heard a man scream like that. Before or since."

Traz hardly breathed. "A wish," he said—a whisper mostly to himself. "She granted him a wish, didn't she? Why else would she do that?" So it *was* real. All of it. Relief washed through him and nearly brought tears to his eyes. He hadn't left Brin for a fool's errand.

Nelson looked at him like he had grown three heads. "Does dying on a blade sound like a wish to you?"

Traz took in the keep's shell. Dark, looming, mournful, and shattered. Stone didn't come apart like that on its own. "What happened?"

Nelson pursed his lips, frustration pulling tight at his scarred face. "I think I've told you too much."

He moved to leave, But Traz caught his sleeve. "Nelson, *please.*"

Nelson sighed, fingers twitching as an unintelligible grumble bubbled from his throat. He adjusted the sword around his waist and settled back into place, "The demoness spoke her vile tongue and darkness gathered around her servant. Blinding white flames burst from her sword and engulfed him. My guards tried to stop her, but her dragon mowed them down." He rubbed his eyes as if rubbing away the impressions of the dead men. "In the chaos, the demoness removed her sword, and the servant was on his feet again. There was this...*presence* about him. Something otherworldly." A shudder ran through Nelson. "We should have run, but we didn't. Before we got our wits about us, though, his mistress gifted her sword to him. He turned into pure terror."

Traz's eyes widened. His heart thumped wildly. "The sword can really do that?"

Nelson's features darkened. "Does that sound *appealing*?"

Traz clutched at the knotted trouser leg beneath his stump. "If it can do that, then..."

"Then what?" Nelson's voice was gruff and hollow.

"I...I have" The words turned to lead into his throat. He couldn't say them—couldn't tell this perfect stranger that the sickness that had taken his leg would eventually take his life, too. That he was afraid to die. That he was afraid to leave Brin alone.

"A wish?" Nelson asked, his voice flat. Another shudder ran through him, and he tucked his chin to his chest, muttering something again.

"*Yes,*" Traz said. "That wish is my only hope. The sword can help me, can't it?"

"No."

Traz's heart stopped in his chest. "What do you mean, no? It brought a *man* back to *life!*"

"And killed *three-hundred men* in a matter of minutes!" He pointed to the pit, then spread his arms wide, taking in the blackened surroundings. "It did *this.* The demoness escaped on her dragon, raining hellfire on us, and left her servant to do as he pleased to cover her escape." Nelson gestured to himself, to the scars and mutilations. "Her servant destroyed *everyone.* He lost his mistress's sword in his deranged state, but still continued to slaughter. I was the *only* one left alive. It's been nothing but a curse." He picked at the leathery, burnt flesh on his arm. "I stay here to discourage others from treading on *his* territory. They won't listen. Never will. Say I'm the fool. But who's the one that's survived this cursed place longer than anyone else?" His eyes roved the burnt stands of trees, as if searching for the demoness' servant. He came back to Traz, his face impassive. "The sword does not grant wishes. It claims sacrifices. And in the end, all it gives it will take again, tenfold. The *wish* you seek is nothing but a lie."

"You don't mean that." Traz couldn't feel his fingers. The blood had drained from them and raced to his face.

"I do," Nelson said without remorse. "Wishes and magic cannot bring you riches and influence and immortal life. If they could, do you think I would be in this pile of death, looking the way I do?"

"No. *No!*" Traz shuffled back a few steps, chest heaving. "You're lying to me. It *has* to be real—" He stopped. Burning realization dawned on him. "It is real. It *is*, and you *know* it is, because you're looking for it yourself, aren't you?"

"Don't have to look when I already know where it is." He drew the sword at his side, just enough for Traz to see it. A hilt with two dragon heads on the finger guards, their sapphire eyes glittering. The grip was made of pale, twisted unicorn horn. Power swirled around it, and whispers reached for Traz. Another shudder ran through Nelson.

Traz looked at him, mouth agape. He couldn't stop shaking. "That's...that's *it*?" Something took him over. Swelled in his muscles and joints. Rage? Fear? Lust? He leapt for the sword, his crutch forgotten in the dirt. A scream tore from his throat. *"Give it to me!"*

Nelson clubbed him across the sternum with his arm. Traz fell back, winded and gasping.

Something changed in Nelson. He sheathed the sword, chest puffed out and shoulders flung back. He reared his head back, glaring down the length of his nose at Traz. The rims around his eyes glowed a deep shade of purple. Lightning arced across his skin, jolting Traz and making his mouth buzz. "You *dare* challenge the sorcerer that brought about T'elemeth's fall?"

Traz fell back farther, heart frozen in his chest, terrified not only of Nelson, but whatever had seemed to take over his body. "You —*what?*"

Nelson took a step closer, the lightning now coalescing into a single, swirling orb. A perfect, miniature storm hanging suspended between his palms. "Listen close, Traz, for I will only tell you this once. I have *no need* for tricks—for mind games. I was taught to kill, and I do it well. You cannot stand against me..." he twitched again and muttered some more. His eyes widened and his magic dissipated. He took a step back, shaking his arms and his face pale. "And *I* cannot stand against the demon, or the power that whispers from this sword. Not for long." He took in the breadth of the plains before him. "I stayed here to bury my friends and all the fools that came after them throwing their lives away for a lie." He looked Traz in the eyes, steel gray to brown. "Please do not become one of them."

Traz couldn't stop heaving for air. His crutch threatened to tremble from his hands. Sweat tumbled down his brow as more voices whispered in his mind. "I won't listen to this anymore," He couldn't tell who he said that to. He staggered back, chest heaving. Nelson tried to approach him, but Traz spat at his feet. "You *are* crazy. I don't know what sword that is, but it's not the one I'm after." It couldn't be. *Wouldn't* be. The sword he was looking for could heal and mend and save. Not take over his mind and body so quickly, like a monstrous parasite. He had to believe that. "I'm *going* to have my wish. Try to stop me and see what happens."

Nelson sighed. "It won't be I, Traz, that tries to stop you. The demon abides no one trying to steal what's his. As soon as the fires go out like candles being squelched, and a single keening note breaks the night, you'll know he's upon you."

Traz fled, skidding and slipping through the corpse moss and tripping over crumbling walls.

"I will be here to help you, Traz, should you survive the night."

Traz didn't care. He had to get away. Away from the madness. Away from the soul-crushing truth he refused to believe. The wish *was* real. It *was*. And not even a sorcerer could convince him otherwise.

When he hobbled back to the others, shaking, steaming, and begging for some sense in the world, no one acknowledged him. Not even Troth, who had set his sights on someone else to terrorize. Just as well. Traz couldn't say what sort of control he had over himself; he was just as liable to break into tears as he was to break a man's jaw.

Traz couldn't get the shaking under control. It was almost as if he could feel the sickness clawing itself up from his missing leg, gouging deep furrows of death in his bones as it made its way to his heart. Death was not far off for him. It lurked in the shadows, waiting to turn his own body against him. And now, the one thing that could help him care for Brin...

Traz shook his head. *No!* It *had* to be real. There was no other option for him. No other option for Brin, alone and penniless, waiting for Traz to return.

Ambrose wandered back over to them, smile pulled too tight against his lips. He bowed to Dravek, the bells on his tassels jingling. They reminded Traz of Nelson's demon repellent, and his mood soured even more. *Stupid, crazy geezer.*

"A song for a coin?" the bard asked Dravek.

"Of course." Dravek motioned him to a seat and called the men over. They gathered around, elbows on knees and eyes wide with ale-soaked wonder.

Ambrose clasped his hands in front of him and leaned forward with them. "I offer an older song of T'elemeth, and the sword that rests here." He glanced at Traz, the milk-white of his eyes stark against the fire's gold. "You there. What is your wish?"

Traz sneered at him and turned away. "To be left alone."

He chuckled, a sound somehow devoid of any warmth. A perfect performer in all but feeling. "Your wish is my duty, young master." He tuned his instrument, the plucked strings making Traz's teeth ache, and then began his song, low and strained and melancholy.

> *Sword of feather*
> *Sword of bone*
> *Cursed be thy wielder*
> *Lest thy wielder be they born*
>
> *Sword of darkness*
> *Sword of love*
> *The lives you reap*
> *Be the lives you keep*

A deep bone shudder ran through Traz, clawing icy tendrils through his chest. He'd never heard this song before, but it shot through his heart like an arrow. All he heard were Nelson's words, ringing like a death knell. *The sword does not grant wishes. It claims sacrifices. And in the end, all it gives it will take again, tenfold.*

> *Sword of Mother*
> *Sword of Daughter*
> *The Ancient Laws you tear apart*
> *To bring back life from whence it starts.*
>
> *Sword of curses*
> *Sword of pain*
> *Lost to prisoners' ruins*
> *By prisoner's pow'r*

The fine hairs along the back of Traz's neck prickled. He looked to the ruins, looming like the spines of a massive beast. No sign of Nelson. But something was out there. Watching. Waiting.

> *Sword of shadow*
> *Sword of mist*
> *The servant searches*
> *With madness as friend*
>
> *Sword of power*
> *Sword of night*
> *To your mistress one day you'll return*
> *And together the world will burn*

The first fire went out. So quick and subtle Traz almost missed it. There was no warning. No last-minute whispers. No shuffling as men climbed into their bedrolls. It was simply silent, as if someone had stomped a firefly. Silent with a single, fading note. Traz almost didn't notice it, except for a brief pause in the bard's song at the exact moment. An odd sort of... mist?... seemed to trail from his skin. A trick of the firelight. It must have been. Traz hugged his crutch to his chest, trying to breathe even as his heart beat a drumming warning in his chest.

Run. Run. Run.

It was fine. It was late. Men were going to put out fires and sleep. It was the way of things. Perfectly reasonable. Perfectly normal. No hidden monsters waiting to pounce in the night.

But then the next one went out at another pause. Closer this time. No preamble. No dying down to a gentle glow. No hiss of steam as water and dirt were thrown over it. Just a keening note; something unearthly moaning in pain. The fire had been there one moment and gone the next, silent as a graveyard.

Like a candle gone out.

The bard smiled and continued with his tune. Traz bolted upright faster than he ever had in his life, missing limb and all. No. Nelson couldn't have been right. He *couldn't* have. But Traz didn't dare gamble his life on his pride. He heaved himself to Dravek, who was sharing another drink with Troth while they listened to the bard. "Dravek, I need to speak with you. *Now.*"

Dravek waved him aside without so much as a sideways glance. "Not now, boy."

Traz pushed Dravek's dismissal aside and gripped his arm. "*Now,* sir."

The bard glanced at Dravek, an odd light in his clouded eyes. "You should listen to the boy." A smile too stiff pulled at his face.

Dravek's lips pursed. "And you have outstayed your coin."

The bard shared a look with Traz. An odd, unfeeling look that froze Traz where he stood. The bard blinked, and the moment ended. He helped himself to a mug of ale without another word.

Dravek stood with a scowl and turned to Traz, towering at least a head-and-a-half over him. "Consider yourself blessed that you're not worth my time. Otherwise, you'd be pulp where you stood for speaking to me that way."

Traz was too terrified of the monster in the dark to be afraid of the one before him. "The demon. It's here."

Troth shouldered his way into the conversation. "Oh? And what makes you the expert in such things?"

Traz ignored him. "Dravek, there's something out there. The other fires are going out." Even as he spoke, another fire went out without so much as a puff of smoke, leaving an empty, soundless void in its place.

Troth laughed and slapped Dravek on the back. "Hear that? Poor tyke's scared of the dark!"

Nelson's voice played in his mind. *They won't listen. Never will. Say I'm the fool. But who's the one that's survived this cursed place longer than anyone else?* Traz knew he sounded ridiculous. He had called Nelson crazy, and now here he was. Guilt battered him in the chest. Frustrated tears welled in his eyes. "*No!* I'm telling you! Something is *out there!* We have to leave! Now!"

"And now he's *cryin'!*" The group roared with Troth's own laughter. "Don't worry! We can keep the fire goin' *all night* just so you can sleep, wee lad!"

Traz leveled a glare at him, a lump of helplessness in his throat. "Troth, you have a family at home, don't you? I'm trying to make sure you get *back to them!*"

"Who are *you* to tell me how to get back to my family?" Troth curled his lip and spat at Traz's feet. "I don't need *your* help, weakling. I'll do just fine when I come home to them with barrels of coin behind me."

Traz ignored him. He knew they would never listen to him. But they respected Dravek. If he listened, they would follow. Traz looked to Dravek, hoping—*praying*—that at least *he* would listen to reason. "You said yourself that hundreds of men have died here. Wouldn't it stand to reason that *something* is killing them?" Another fire went out. This time, Traz heard a single strangled cry.

Dravek didn't. He waved him off and turned away. "Nothing but pure greed that killed those fools. I don't ascribe to ghost stories, boy, and neither should you."

"But you'll trust a legend about a sword that *grants wishes?*" Traz tried to drag him back. "Dravek, unless we go *right now*, all of you are going to *die!*"

The blow came in a single explosion of anger, catching Traz off guard and leaving him sprawled on the ground. His crutch skittered away from him, and his head and cheek throbbed. Dravek loomed, heaving in breathless anger over him. "We were *dying* at home, too! What shall we tell your brother when he falls to the sickness and finds out his brother abandoned the one thing that could save him?"

Traz reeled back, the words more devastating than any blow, the shadows of his parents last footsteps echoing in his mind. No, not Brin. He couldn't fall sick. *Wouldn't.*

"I lost my wife to the sickness. And if it hadn't been that, it would have been starvation. I will gladly face the Pit itself before I let others die like her, and before the kingdom goes unpunished for its silence." Dravek kicked Traz's crutch over to him. It thwacked him on the brow. "Leave my sight, filthy coward. If I ever see you again, a demon will be the least of your worries." He grabbed Traz by the shirtfront and pulled him to eye level. "And if you get in my way tomorrow, there will be so little left of you that even the crows won't bother." Dravek threw him back to the ground and kicked a cloud of dust in his face.

Traz didn't see their fire go out. Only a curled, unearthly smile on the bard's face as black mist curled from his skin. One moment, the roaring warmth of the fire singed Traz's skin. The next, gooseflesh erupted across his arms as a deep, bone-numbing cold fell with the curtain of darkness. Almost as one, bodies dropped to the ground. Troth fell at Traz's foot. Dravek collapsed across Traz, sightless eyes wide-open, still filled with spitting hate. A keening note held suspended over the air, shattering the night, before it fell silent once more.

Traz screamed and shoved the corpse away. The sound seemed muted somehow. Unreal and unearthly. Traz couldn't suck in breath. His shirt felt too tight for his chest, clawing up his throat and strangling him. He saw Dravek. Then his parents. Same eyes. Dull and without spark. Blood pooling behind them as droplets spilled from their mouth. Traz shoved his knuckles into his mouth to keep from screaming. *Not again. Not again!*

Something laughed out in the darkness—or at least, what Traz could only assume was a laugh. It was a sound that flooded the inky darkness, hissing like the tide washing out to sea. Implacable. Unstoppable. "Tell the others, boy, that T'elemeth belongs to me, the servant of Mother Night's last priestess. This is the fate of those that trespass." And then it appeared.

The demon.

The *bard*.

The bright clothes melted into frayed brown robes, and its skin lost all color save for the twisting, undulating markings across its face. Drenched in wisps of dark energy—*magic*—it looked at Traz with those horrible eyes, sharpened teeth pulling apart in a sadistic, twisted grin. "You wished to be alone, maggot. I grant you your wish. Their deaths are enough to make my mistress' weapon sing. There is no reason to save you from your chosen despair." And then it swept away onto the plain, toward the other unsuspecting fires.

The weight of the air lifted as soon as it left. The darkness' grip on his chest eased. But the guilt did not. *Had* he wished for this? His words to the bard—bitter and ignorant—came back to him from across that fire.

What is your wish, boy?

To be left alone.

But *was* it his fault? Or had the demon meant to kill them anyway? The thoughts and guilt piled on him and threatened to suffocate him, but he shoved them aside for now. He had to. It was the only way he could survive for Brin.

Traz sat in a horrified daze for more time than he knew how to keep. What did he do now? Would...*it* be back? Bile rose to the back of his throat as his heart rammed his ribcage. How could he *dare* to think he would survive, surrounded by all these men that had fallen in one swoop, without sound or warning? This was the end, wasn't it? He was a sitting, one-legged duck out here. The demon would shred him to pieces the moment it came back, and—

He dug his fingertips into his eyebrows, trying to drive the panic away. He couldn't think like that. Not with Brin waiting for him to come home. He had to do something. Find some help.

I will be here to help you, Traz, should you survive the night.

Traz shakily gathered himself and took one last look across the group. The moon finally peeked its face from behind clouds and cast skeletal shadows across their faces. Traz's heart quailed. So many families were now without husbands, brothers, sons, and fathers. All for a single wish.

Traz left them there, their phantoms permanently etched in his mind.

Traz found Nelson almost exactly where he left him, staring out over the valley. Only half the fires remained now. Traz couldn't think about the other faces gathered around them, waiting for a morning that would never come.

"It's an unnatural feeling, isn't it?" Nelson asked without looking at Traz. "Watching people die from the very thing you warned them about. A danger they could have avoided if they only believed you."

Traz couldn't shake the skeletal shadows from his mind. "Nelson, I'm sorry. I shouldn't have—I *should*—"

Nelson raised a hand and cut him off. "Shoulds serve no purpose but to let you wallow in self-pity. I should know. I failed my duty the night that demon freed his mistress, and I've spent the last thirty-years trying to make it right."

Traz had no response to that. He swallowed back his tears and nodded.

"Good. We can grieve and atone later. For now, we have a demon to stop, and with you're help, I think I may have a plan that will work."

A scream punctured the night and the sword at Nelson's side thrummed a wailing note. Traz jumped and nearly lost his crutch. The scream died almost instantly, strangled in a gurgling throat. The sword's note did not.

"Poor fool's faster than most. He got a chance to try to run," Nelson mused. "Almost a mercy to die not knowing what's killing you."

"That was close to here." Traz could hardly get the sound out.

"Let's go. There's work to be done. Let's build ourselves a fortress."

Traz's faith in Nelson deteriorated with each new wall that went up on their "fortress". Nelson had buried the wailing sword in the back corner and built a shoddy pile of debris around it. The keening never stopped. Traz dragged a rotting pallet over to their haphazard lump of broken wall and old barrels and then stood aside to give Nelson a dubious look. "Nelson, I don't think this will be sturdy enough to keep a demon out."

He took a step too far and Nelson gripped his arm. "The traps! We don't have time to be mucking about!" Nelson opened their "doorway" and motioned Traz inside. "It will do. Get in before we're out of time."

Traz scrambled inside and crammed as far into the corner as he could to allow room for Nelson. Nelson crouched down, eyes boring into Traz's. He was quiet for a time, and then asked. "You really would do anything for this brother of yours, wouldn't you? Even face down a demon?"

Traz furrowed his brow, unsure where the question was supposed to lead. "Of course."

Nelson smiled, his muscles straining beneath his thick scars. He leaned back and took in the swathe of muted moonlight. "My brother said the same thing before he died. He shielded me from the worst of a fire blast. Couldn't save my face, though." He laughed, and then wiped a few tears away. "It'd be nice to see him again." He tossed something to Traz. Traz caught it, and it jangled softly in his hand. Nelson's demon repellent. "Only enough magic for one person to be protected by that bell, and I'm done watching people add their bones to this rotting crypt."

It took Traz two blinks to register what Nelson had said. When he did, his eyes went wide. "Wait, Nelson! No!" He rushed to the entrance, but Nelson had already shut him in. He tried to claw through the debris, but magical wards kept him tucked away inside. He had just enough leeway to catch Nelson by the arm. "There has to be another way! We can hide together and wait 'til morning!"

Nelson smiled again. He patted Traz on the arm. "Thirty years experience has taught me that there aren't as many options as we think." He spoke a few words, and a spell climbed up Traz's arm and covered his mouth. Traz tried to protest, but no sound came out. "You're young and willing to change. And, most importantly, you're willing to help others do the same. That's more than I could ever say for my sorry self." He pulled his arm from Traz's grip. "Whatever you do, take care of your family. And above all else, do not let that demon have his sword."

The last fire went out.

The sword's throbbing note grew in pitch and intensity and rang in Traz's ears. Time stretched far beyond its normal limits. Traz felt nearly crushed by the nothingness beyond the sword's sound. His heart battered him. Nelson let go of him and moved out into the open. Traz couldn't tell if it was moments or hours later when a disembodied voice shattered the stillness.

"I know you."

The demon materialized in front of Nelson, bathed in silver moonlight.

"You have hidden well these thirty years. Where is your protection now?" The instant it opened its mouth, Traz's heart twisted in knots in his chest. His head pounded with adrenaline and abject terror. He couldn't tell if he was breathing anymore. Dravek's and Troth's and all the other men's faces swam in his mind.

The demon craned its neck to take in its surroundings, as a tyrant would survey his domain. Traz covered his mouth to keep from screaming.

The demon caught Nelson by the throat, long, wicked nails carving furrows into his skin, and hoisted him off his feet. Nelson choked and struggled uselessly against the demon's grip. The demon touched Nelson's face with its free hand, exploring every crevice and scar. It laughed, the sound so quiet but penetrating that it shook the ground beneath Traz. "You've changed, my friend. Who has hurt you so?"

In response, Nelson spit in its face.

The demon didn't flinch. Instead, it grinned. It was the most horrifying contortion of a face Traz had ever seen. "Grudges never die, do they?" The grin dropped off the demon's face in an instant. "I thought I killed you."

Nelson choked out a laugh. "You thought wrong."

The demon's nostrils flared, and its milky eyes flashed scarlet. "Where is the sword? I heard it's cries for me, but you have hidden them." It shook Nelson. "I cannot return to my mistress without her sword!"

Traz glanced to the sword. How could the demon not hear it?

"Why? She betrayed you. She took every bit of humanity from you."

The demon scoffed bitterly. "*Betrayed* me, you say? She gave me life. I have all the power I could ever want."

Traz's heart clenched again. He thought of Troth. Of Dravek. Dead where they stood.

Nelson chuckled. "Except for her sword."

The demon's jaw twitched. It dug its talon-like fingernails deeper into Nelson's neck, drawing small beads of blood. "My mistress gave me a place. I need that sword to claim it."

Nelson tsked. "Not really belonging... when you have to... pay for a seat at the table."

The demon growled. "Spare me your sermons. I have no need for them. Tell me where to find the sword!"

Nelson cackled. "Thirty years... and you think an old... burnt husk can find it better than... an *all-powerful* demon? Does your... mistress know you... doubt... the power she... gave you?"

Traz's mouth was as dry as old parchment. He licked his lips and clenched sweat-slicked palms around the bell. What did that crazy old man think he was doing? He was going to get himself killed!

The demon's lip curled up in a snarl. "You don't have it, do you?"

Nelson cracked a smile. "Nope."

The demon smiled. "Then your use has ended."

A flash. An explosion of dark mist.

Traz screamed as Nelson fell. No blood. No gore. One moment, he was struggling against the demon's hand on his throat. The next, he was limp. Broken. Shattered on the ground. Just like the others.

Traz shocked himself when the sound broke through his throat. He clutched it, angry tears pouring down his face. Of course the spell had broken. Its caster was dead.

And the sword keened into the night.

The demon looked up, milk-white eyes scanning the ruins, darting sightlessly back and forth. A smile tore at its lips. "There you are." It moved toward the sword.

Traz snatched it. A flood of voices scoured his mind the moment he touched it; hissing, whispering, screaming all at once. For blood. For vengeance. For rescue. Traz staggered back and nearly dropped it. Was *that* what Nelson had heard every moment that sword had been strapped to his waist? How did he string coherent thoughts together?

The demon's smile vanished. "So, the worthless sorcerer has a friend, does he? Keeping my prize from me now, too, are you? Show yourself, wretch!"

He cannot hear me when you hold both me and that silver bell. The sword's voices coalesced into one that hissed through his mind, soft and goading.

"What do you mean?" Traz muttered before he could help himself.

The demon whirled toward the sound. Traz froze and didn't dare to breathe.

The bell is enchanted. It repels demons and their dark magic, and protects all that touch it from their detection.

Traz would have breathed a sigh of relief if he didn't fear the demon would hear that, too.

This is your chance, Traz. Run away with me now, and I will grant you anything you wish.

"*Show yourself!*" the demon shrieked.

Traz did. His feet moved of their own accord to the fortress' entrance. Was he the one doing that, or the sword? It didn't matter. He clawed his way out of the fortress and stood before the demon, head held proud and bell clutched tightly to his chest. Every inch of him quivered with rage and guilt. His fault. His fault he had left Brin alone. His fault he couldn't convince the others to run. His fault Nelson had to give up his protection. But not his fault that they were dead. This demon still had their blood on its hands.

And Traz couldn't let it touch anyone else.

The demon whirled at the sound of the hideaway collapsing and charged, robes billowing about it and magic poisoning the air. Traz braced for impact, but it never came. Instead, mere inches shy of reaching Traz, a light flashed, and the demon whirled away, screaming as if burned. The bell glowed fiercely in Traz's hand. The demon howled some more and glowered in Traz's direction. "That *wretch!*"

Traz looked at the bell in awe. It really *was* demon repellent. He looked at Nelson's crumpled body and tightened his grip on the bell.

And Nelson had given it to him - a perfect stranger - willingly. Traz had to repay that sacrifice.

The sword buzzed in his hand. His body shook and his vision hazed around the edges, scarlet tinged with black. The sword pulled at his arm, yearning toward its master, but Traz drew it back. He had a plan. He thought. He hoped. A stupid plan just like the ones he had promised Brin he wouldn't use. If Nelson's bell worked, then Traz had to trust that everything else did as well.

"I have your sword!"

The demon screeched with a sound no human could ever achieve and charged at him. Traz slammed back with the bell's wall of protection. The demon yowled and lashed out, but its claws raked past Traz's face without touching him. Another burst of light, and the demon's howl turned into an ear shattering shriek as it stumbled away.

Traz ran. Or ran as best he could, shambling through the ruins at pell-mell pace. He didn't remember where Nelson had led him. But if he squinted close enough against the moonlight, he saw the tracks Nelson had worn down over his thirty years through the black moss and dried grasses. And somewhere between them, traps awaited.

I will lead you, the sword said. *You and I will rule this land together.*

The demon followed Traz, stalking like a wolf, nose to the air and ears tuned for the barest noise. It kept its distance from Traz and the bell, but its eyes burned with silver, raging fire.

"Thirty years, and it's been under your nose this whole time!" Traz said, goading it closer still. "What would your mistress think?"

The demon screamed, combusting in fury. "I will have my prize, pest! You do not know the thousands I've killed. A worm is nothing to me."

"Kill me, then! Or has a lowly sorcerer beaten you?"

"I have beaten him! Who is the one that lies dead in the ashes of his failure?"

"And who continues to fail?" Traz didn't know where this stupid, unhinged bravery came from. Nelson, probably. Just batty enough to be genius. He hoped he could do him justice.

"ENOUGH!" The demon launched itself at Traz, wreathed in blinding white flames and speaking in a hissing, guttural language that Traz had no intention of understanding.

Let me guide you, the sword said. *One step to the left is all you need.*

Traz's body moved on its own. One step too far. He snagged a circle of bells, and the trap sprung on him like monster jaws snapping shut. The jolt and pain and blinding light shot through him at once. He kept his grip on the sword, but lost the bell. The sword laughed in his mind.

Traz fell beneath the demon's weight as it collided with him. His chin struck the ground and his brain clattered in his skull. He lost focus in his eyes and saw only the vague shapes of the demon's markings. Its claws dug and ripped into Traz's skin as it crawled up his body, dragging itself blindly toward the sword.

Traz cried out and scrambled for the lost bell, but the demon took his head into its palm and ground his face into the gravel. "Do you know how many I have killed for this sword? You are *nothing*, and will die as nothing."

"I'm...*not*...going to die here," Traz said, voice gasping through the pain.

The demon wrapped its fingers over the sword hilt, the other hand prying Traz's away from the grip. In that shared touch, Traz saw nothing but nightmares. Rivers of blood seeping deep into the soil. Legions marching against each other, their blades ringing with death. Mountains collapsing. Villages burning. Great, white wings blotting out the sky and leaving a lifeless world behind.

Traz screamed and flung himself to the side, dislodging both of them from the weapon. Traz snatched it and fumbled for the bell. Where was it? Where *was* it? His hand brushed the cool silver just as the demon flung a roaring, searing wall of magic at him. It turned the crumbling walls and carrion moss to ash and left a deep furrow in the earth behind it.

Traz braced himself against the impact, clutching the bell to his chest. He thought of Brin. And prayed.

The wall exploded, filling the air with crackling fractures of lightning and magic as it arced around Traz. The impact sent him flying back into a broken, charred tree, the bell burning so hot in his hand it left a brand. The hollow bark collapsed around him, and the impact left him with white spots flooding his vision and a ringing in his ears. He'd dropped the sword.

For a moment, the rush of adrenaline and nausea and blinding lights drowned out everything else. And then, as his senses returned to him, so did the screaming.

Traz picked himself out of the tree and felt around for his crutch, every inch of him begging to be put out of its misery. He found the crutch in shambles, shattered against a rock. So instead, he found a gnarled branch and hobbled his way back to the demon, every inch of him screaming to run, to hide, to, sweet Mother Night, *stop* so he could tend to his wounds. But he didn't. He pressed on and found a pathetic sight.

The demon screamed and howled in a cage made of string and bells, tears pouring down its face as it tried to reach for the sword. Mere centimeters from its clawed fingertips.

Traz approached, and it seemed to sense him. It looked at him, its face screwed up in the most horrific mask of rage and hatred and malice. "One day," it seethed, "I will find you without that protection, and that is the day you find out what genuine pain is. I will take great pleasure in educating you."

"And who will come to release something like you?"

It smiled in its inhuman way. "Greed and power will always seek us out wherever we may rest."

"Feel free to rest here as long as you like." Traz picked up the sword and implanted into the ground, just tantalizingly close enough to drive the demon mad. "I'll make sure no one comes to find you." He walked away with its howls ringing in his ears just as the first rays of morning light peeked over the ruins.

It was only when the demon was out of sight that Traz's body quaked, as if all his bones might come undone. The only thing keeping him upright was his crutch. The plains and ruins swam before him in dizzying, muddy colors. He bent over and retched, emptying his stomach of absolutely everything. Not that there was much there to begin with.

Lightheaded and dizzy, he made his way back to Nelson. Tears and great, heaving sobs threatened in his chest as he passed the doused fires and the bodies beside them. He couldn't think of that now. It was too much. He averted his eyes and tried to push their glaring, accusing faces to the back of his mind. But they lingered. There would be time enough to bury them. But Nelson, of all of them, deserved the first proper send off.

Traz's eyes watered at the thought. Why? Why had that stupid old man risked everything just to save him?

Traz limped to the body. It hardly looked real. More like a broken rag doll left abandoned in the dirt. He eased to the ground, tears falling, and checked for signs of life. He knew there would be none, but he had to try.

"Chasing him...down like a love hungry...bull. Never thought of that."

Traz leapt back, heart in his throat. It couldn't be. How...? What...? "Nelson! I thought...but you were—" It didn't matter. He was *alive*!

"Don't...celebrate just...yet. I'm not long for...here..."

Traz helped Nelson sit up a bit. The older man's breath wheezed in his chest, and his limbs quivered feebly. Every movement seemed to cause him great pain. "What are you talking about? Use your magic!"

"Magic won't save me...this time." He patted Traz's hand. "As the Ancient Laws...say. The dead...must...remain with...the dead."

Traz's hold tightened on him. "But you're not dead yet." Even though every word sounded like the greatest effort Nelson could muster. Even though his heart beat slower with each moment. Traz knew the sound of a dying man. That didn't mean he had to like it any better.

Nelson smiled, his gray eyes glittering in the sunlight. "You're right. Still have time enough...to do...one thing." He haltingly ground out a few words Traz didn't understand — the language of magic. A floating orb appeared in his hand, glowing bluish purple and swirling with energy. Traz let out a sigh of relief. Nelson had enough magic to heal himself. Traz bowed his head, sending a silent thank you to whatever gods would hear him.

"What was...your wish...Traz?"

Traz shook his head. "Doesn't matter anymore. I won't come near that sword again."

"Tell...me..."

A bitter tear of disappointment slid down Traz's face. He should have known. Nothing in this life came free. Even so, he... "I wanted to be healed," he said, fighting back a lump in his throat. "I wanted to take care of my brother!" The tears spilled then. Hot and fast as he choked on his emotions. "And now...he'll have to watch me die. Just like I've watched everyone else die. I just...I wanted to protect him!" He covered his face in his tunic and wept. His parents. Dravek. Even Troth. All the men dead on those plains. They would haunt him until the day he died. And now, whether or not he wanted it, he would haunt Brin one day. And leave him all alone to live with those nightmares.

"You've done well, Traz."

Traz shook his head, still hidden in his tunic.

"Look...at...me..."

Traz did, and Nelson's magic blinded him as he pressed it into his face. It absorbed into his skin—raced through his veins like freezing fire—and the pain from his illness stopped. The creeping fingers of death vanished.

Nelson slumped against him, hacking and wheezing, his entire body wracked with each breath.

Traz tried to drag him upright again, shock freezing his tears in their place. "What did you— that was for you!"

"Slowed...sickness. Not gone...but...you...should live...long time, now."

Traz blinked. "Wh—what?"

Nelson smiled again, every gap in his teeth prominent. He patted Traz's hand. "Say...'lo to...Brin. Take care of...him."

More tears than Traz ever thought possible spilled down his face. He *felt* it. Felt himself gaining years back that he never thought he would have. Words failed. How did he possibly convey his gratitude for the gift Nelson had given him? "Why? Why *me*?"

Nelson curled his fist around the bell, still in Traz's hand. "Remind me...of...my brother. Had a...debt...to pay." A laugh gurgled from his throat, even as a tear slid down his mottled cheek.

Traz swiped a hand under his nose and dabbed at his eyes. "You're crazy, old man!" He laughed with Nelson, but his breath hitched in his chest. "How can I even *begin* to thank you?"

Nelson tapped a finger on Traz's chest. "You...be good...kind... protect sword...like you...already have...will have thanked me... tenfold. Promise?"

Traz nodded, feeling wholly inadequate for such trust. "I promise."

"Good." Nelson fell into his final rest, and Traz wailed into the morning dawn. Alone with his demon's wish and a sword he would never use. Healed from his friend's blessing, and with a promise to keep.

DEATH FALLS

Many years after its conception
Loralan fell to Death's fury
He crept through men's hearts
And left honeyed chaos in his footsteps

The neighbors poisoned our withered crops
Only right to steal their coin
The king fed his family while others starved
Only right to claim their lives.

Any atrocity could be twisted into righteousness
When "justice" stood by its side.
Death used and abused this moral line
All for the sake of his ring.

Many turned to frothing monsters
Intent on serving their selfish desires
Death shrouded the kingdom in his billowing storm
And flitted from bloodstain to next.

Innocents withered in the shadow of his search
Beaten and bloodied; starved to mere memories
All save three siblings huddled close
In the ruins of their father's castle

A single ring kept safe in their hands.

"Save our people," pled their mother
Before she swallowed darkest death.
"Never forget your own power."
Their father, drawing last breath.

Two sons and a daughter lived on in their legacy
Their kingdom to save 'gainst Death's madness.
All shy of adult years, adult lives by far.
But their adult fears knew fate never considered such
     things.

To corners of Loralan where the sun still smiled
They fled in search of chaos' cure.
They found it in trust, in love, and loyalty
And allies turned family gathered to their side.

To battle they marched each heart as one
Loathe for the looming violence
But eager to bring the world to right.
And so to Death they took their cause.

That is where all knowledge ceases.
They met Death on the Plain of Kings
He swallowed them in his vengeful maw
And history lost its reckoning.

Whether Death retrieved his stolen ring

Or Man found means to destroy even him
No living soul will ever know
For those who lived it locked their words away, never to be
  spoken or written.

All any can say of this lost day
Is the band returned laid low by the loss of one prince
And Death relinquished his hold upon Loralan
To retreat, weak and broken, to the Phoenix Mountains.

His presence remains there
In a forest bereft of life
Where wails echo from within a cloak of mist
And whispers trail flames of temptation and regret.

Loralan lived on in the wake of its tragedy
Rebuilt on the final threads of peace laid by its forefathers.
They mourned the lost and built shrines to their memory
And life moved on in work, peace, love, community.

Death and his ring faded to whispers in the night.
Time moved on from generation to next
Lives flowed and ebbed
And death eclipsed forgotten Death.

WISDOM OF THE IMMORTAL

Man reaches for eternity like moths to flame
Tempted by beauty that scorches their wings
Long life
Legacy
Power
Anything to keep the barest idea of their existence in our
  mortal realm.

They do not realize
Eternity is not meant for imperfect soil.
In its bloom lies only ruin
One year too many poisons the mind
One crack too great, the monument crumbles
Men wage wars and build lifetimes
'Round immortality
When all that waits is golden ash.

Eternity for this mortal realm
Is not in endless years or lofty deeds.

It is in your love's eyes
When the world stops and the stars open wider and
  brighter
To magnify your heart's brilliance.
It is in a child's laugh
When you feel their wonder and cradle it
Tucked away with yours; the one you're told to hide.
It is in music,
Transcending race, language, and grudge,
And brings all together for one more dance.

Eternity blooms in quiet moments
When all is joy and peace and love
Enjoy each breath spent near her heart
For eternity is as fleeting
As dandelions in spring.

UNDER THE COUNTER

Abran remembered the first time he saw an elf. They had emerged from the mists of the Woods of Desolation, regal and proud as magic swirled in their green eyes. He had gaped, open-mouthed, at them for so long that his mother had to reach over and close his mouth for him. They had been so tall, so mysterious in their billowing cloaks and their long, silky hair. They seemed perfect—above the woes of any human existence. And six-year-old Abran's heart filled to bursting with curiosity and wonder at the sight of them.

Nearly twenty years later, the elves still traveled from the Golden Grove and made stops in Alvernet on their way to the rest of their journeys. They still brought with them that air of benevolent other-worldliness that was somehow both comforting and maddening. All of them did, except for the woman now perusing his shop.

"Do you make these all yourself?" she asked, trailing her long fingers over the leather work on the shelves and hanging on the walls. Bridles, bracers, bags, aprons, pelts—they had it all. Abran knew each piece by heart, and watching her brush across them almost felt like someone peering into his soul.

Abran fumbled with the rag he'd been using to polish a single spot on his counter. The spot gleamed conspicuously against the rest of the worn and decidedly *un*-polished sections. "Uh...*yes*. Yes, I did. Well, most of them, I suppose. My father still dabbles every now and again. When the arthritis will let him, of course." He was babbling. Oh, Sister *Earth* he was babbling. What was he supposed to *say* to someone with infinite power, wisdom, and years to live? He had gone his whole life without truly interacting with a single one of them, let alone one that was in his shop, chatting just as easily as if they'd been neighbors for years.

The elf had leaned her elbow on the counter, her chin resting on her hand while her long, chestnut hair as fine as silk cascaded over her shoulder and pooled on his counter. Her large, slanted eyes the color of lily stems danced with amusement. She said nothing— simply watched him flounder.

"Can I help you find something?" Abran asked with a mortifying squeak.

A smile turned the corner of her mouth. She looked around the shop conspiratorially. "No, but I could use your help with something else."

Blessedly, some of Abran's sense came back to him. Elves were not the only people to pass through Alvernet. He'd seen his fair share of thieves and conmen, too—often coming in with a favor to ask to get him to drop his guard before striking. It would stand to reason that at least *one* elf might have ascribed to that same lifestyle. No matter how beautiful and mysterious she might have been.

Abran threw his polishing rag over his shoulder and folded his arms over his chest. "Depends," he said, his voice thankfully squeak-free this time.

The elf straightened, her hair catching the light of the single window above his shop door and turning to copper. "In about five minutes, another elf is going to walk through those doors looking for me. Where's the best place for me to hide?" She gave him a wry, apologetic look.

Abran lowered his arms, his eyebrows drawn up in bewilder-ment. That had certainly been the first time he'd heard *that.* "You're not in trouble with the law, are you?"

She laughed, a pure, clear sound that drew a smile from Abran despite himself. "If my sister has her way, then eventually I might be, but today, I'm no criminal. Simply desperate to shake an unwelcome escort."

Abran pursed his lips and gave her a narrow look. He wasn't sure if he was even *allowed* to say no to an elf. Would she turn him into a duck if he did? He didn't want to find out. "If I find out later that you lied to me, I'll just tell the authorities you bewitched me to suit your own agenda."

She raised an eyebrow. "*Bewitched?* I like the sound of that."

Heat rushed to the tips of Abran's ears. He cleared his throat, casting around for someplace suitable for her to hide. The secret passages behind the stock shelves would have been suitable. But, then, that would have defeated the purpose of 'secret'. There was nothing else for it, then. Abran motioned to beneath his counter. "I used to hide under here as a child when the village bullies were after me. It might be a tight squeeze for a grown adult, but it should work well enough."

She looked him up and down incredulously. "A strong man like you had to run away from a group of boys?"

Abran shrugged his tunic around his shoulders, self-conscious. "I was a *child*," he said. "And those *girls* were relentless."

She winced, a mildly haunted look in her eyes. "Ahh, yes, you're right. Girls are terrifying." She crouched and crawled beneath the counter, curling her knees to her chest, her fine, pointed ears brushing the underside of the wood. Abran blinked dumbly at her for a moment. He hadn't expected her to actually take him up on the ridiculous offer.

She peered up at him. "I don't suppose you have something to help cover the rest of me, do you?"

"Ah, right." No sooner had Abran thrown a cloth drapery over the counter—kept handy in case the counter looked particularly dingy that day—then a pair of elves entered the shop. The elven woman— all slim, sharp lines the color of pale moonlight—let her eyes rove across Abran's shelves, her lip curled in cool disdain. She elbowed the elven man next to her, who even for an elf was remarkably unre- markable, all blank stares and placid nothingness. "Did you see her, Pine?"

Pine shook his head mutely.

The woman scoffed something that sounded like "useless" and approached Abran, walking as gingerly as if the floor were covered in rat droppings. Abran straightened the cloth to make sure it covered his fugitive completely land gave the other woman a tight smile. "What can I do for you today?"

The woman ignored him. Her dark green eyes darted everywhere except his face, probing every nook and shadow as if the shop hid ancient, dark secrets. Abran turned to follow her gaze, where she scowled at a fat spider in the corner.

"M'lady," Abran said. "I can assure you that spider is a much-loved and fully certified apprentice for this shop. He keeps away the moths."

The elven woman turned her incensed look on him and growled in exasperation. "I don't care about the *spider*. Have you seen a woman?"

Abran glanced at the spiderweb again. "I'll admit I don't know much about your culture, but if you don't mind me asking, what would a woman be doing in a spider's web?"

He thought he might have heard the barest snicker beneath his counter.

The elven woman's lips pressed together in a thin, almost translucent line. "Thank you for being an utter waste of my time." She turned on her heel, flaxen hair whipping Abran in the face, and stormed out of the shop.

Pine followed her out. "If your sister doesn't want to meet me, then—"

"Shut. UP. Pine!"

Once the two elves were safely out of earshot, Abran lifted the cloth and raised an eyebrow. "*Sister?*"

The chestnut-haired elf stuck out her hand and Abran helped her out. "Found me out," she said, stretching her back and grimacing. "That's my sister, Inula. She thinks she's doing me a favor by parading around a string of eligible bachelors for me to choose from."

Abran folded the counter cloth and put it back on the shelf. "And I'm assuming you're not interested in any bachelors?"

"It's not that I'm not interested. I'm just not interested in the ones *she* chooses." She leaned back against the counter, eyes as bright as her smile. "I prefer my men...shorter."

Abran wasn't holding anything, but still fumbled his hands as if he was. The tips of his ears burned red hot. He couldn't look her in the eye. "So...*was* there anything you wanted here? Or did I just happen to be a convenient hiding spot?"

"Oh, no, there's definitely something I want." She approached him, her tall, slim form casting shadows over him. Her hair shone amber in the light streaming through the shop front. She stepped so close to him he could feel her breath on his hair. His heart stuttered to a stop. She reached around him, her arm brushing his. "I quite like—" her voice skated across his ear. "This arm guard." She pulled the item off the shelf and held it in front of him. "My niece is an archer."

Abran just gaped at her in a daze for a few minutes before coming to his senses. "Right, *right!* Yes, you're right." He cleared his throat and eyed the piece. "That'll be...3 copper."

She pulled the money from a pouch at her waist and handed it to him. "Thank you." She dropped a few extra coins in his hand. "For everything." She walked to the door—leaving a trailing scent of fresh flowers in her wake—but stopped before exiting. "My name is Calla, by the way—like the lily. Maybe we'll see each other again sometime?"

"Uh-huh," Abran responded dumbly.

She smiled and left with a parting wave.

When she was gone, whatever spell had come over Abran broke as well. He rubbed the back of his neck and scoffed to himself, shaking his head. "I am *never* seeing her again. Tanner's don't get *that* lucky."

ABRAN WHISTLED to himself as he hung brand new, glistening bridles on the hooks near the front of the shop. The sun streamed in through the front windows, warming his back, and he licked his lips to get the last tastes of his mother's apple pie off them. He already regretted eating it so quickly.

"So, I hear you have this extra service where you let customers in need hide under your counter. Is that still available?"

Abran nearly fell off his step stool when he heard Calla's voice. Instead, several bridles fell off their hooks as he used them for balance. He ignored them and cleared his throat. "I'm afraid that's more of a one-time service," he said, trying to sound smooth but his voice cracking slightly as he looked at her in befuddlement. She *had* come back. Why? "Most people feel they've seen too much of this shop once they've been under there."

Calla grinned, her entire face lighting up. "Oh, no. I found it fascinating." She glanced over her shoulder. "Perhaps you could make an exception to your one service per client rule?"

Abran followed her gaze and saw Inula across the street with a different male elf in tow. "You weren't joking that she had a whole string of men for you, were you?"

Calla's face grew pained. "I wish I were." She looked back at him. "She is getting closer, though, so about that hiding space?"

Abran blinked at her a few times before the words settled in. "Oh, right! Right." He grabbed the cloth and threw it over the counter again. She ducked beneath it only moments before Inula forced her presence into the store. Her face tightened in disgust when she saw Abran.

"I don't suppose anyone *else* tends this shop?" she asked. "I'd like to speak with someone that has at least half a brain."

Abran realized too late that the toe of Calla's boot was sticking out from beneath the cloth, right in view of Inula. "Um...nope. No." He moved in front of the counter, banging his thigh on the corner and barely withholding a screech of pain. "Nobody here but me. This is Tanner and Son, and I'm Tanner, and don't have a son yet, so it's just me. My father used to be the Tanner, and I was the son, but then his arthritis and—"

"*Sweet* Mother Night, I *do not* care. Just cease. Speaking." Inula backed out of the shop so quickly she nearly tripped over the elf behind her. "We won't get anywhere with this level of stupidity," she muttered as they left. When they were gone, Abran curled into himself and let out a muffled, frustrated scream as he pressed his palm against what would inevitably be a nasty bruise. "Rotten... table. Stupid corner."

"Are you all right?" Calla's voice floated to him from beneath the cloth, strangled as if holding back laughter.

Abran glowered in her direction, and she poked her head out with a grin. "Have you considered alternative solutions to this problem?" he asked. "Like *talking* to your sister?"

"You think I would stuff myself into a place certainly *not* built for elves if I hadn't tried that already?" She stuck her hand out for help, and he unwedged her from beneath the counter.

"All I'm saying is there *has* to be an easier solution than this."

Calla scoffed and brushed herself off. "With my sister, *nothing* is easy."

"I could believe it," Abran said, perhaps a bit *too* candidly. The fact that she had believed his stupidity act a little *too* quickly smarted at his pride.

Calla laughed. "I promise she's not bad *all* the time. When our parents left, she was there for me, and I can never thank her enough for that." She got a wistful look in her eyes, but then they widened and her hand flew to her mouth. "By the Architects, here I am hiding under your counter and spouting off my whole life story, and I don't even know your *name*!"

He gave her a wry grin, waggling his eyebrows. "I just went over this with your sister. I'm the son from Tanner and son."

She lightly smacked his arm. "No, really! I feel horrible!"

Abran laughed. Her horror was so genuine over such a little thing that he couldn't help it. "Honestly, you bring such a whirlwind with you I hadn't even realized." He swept his arms out and bowed deeply. "Abran Tanner at your service, m'lady."

She smiled sheepishly and curtsied. "It is a pleasure, Sir Tanner."

Abran grimaced. "Just Abran, please."

"Abran," she corrected herself. She glanced out the window,

where the sun still streamed through, and a refreshing breeze wafter through the door. "Will you let me take you on a walk around town as payment for my," she cast her hand around her head as if batting at flies, "whirlwinds?"

"I mean, I'd love to say yes," Abran said. "but won't Inula catch you outside?"

Calla waved her hand dismissively. "Inula hates spending time with humans. If she can't find me within an hour or two, she'll go back to the Golden Grove and just wait for me to come home. If I come back late enough, the suitors will have gone home for the night."

Abran glanced around the shop. "It *has* been a slow day," he said. The sunshine called to him from outside. How long had it been since he had closed early just to enjoy himself? "So if you're sure it won't get you in trouble, then—"

Before he could finish, Calla snagged him by the wrist and dragged him out the door.

ALL THEIR ENCOUNTERS followed a similar pattern after that. Abran wouldn't see Calla for sporadic amounts of time—sometimes a few days, sometimes a few weeks—and then one day she would just be *there*, crawling under his counter as he threw the ratty cloth over it. Inula was always close behind, but never entered the store again, pacing with a huff before leaving. After the fifth such encounter, Calla brought Abran a strawberry tart as a thank you. He took one bite and had to brace himself against the counter.

"What *is* this?"

Calla's normally indomitable smile faltered. "A...strawberry tart?"

Abran took another heaping bite, his eyes closed in ecstasy. "I could *kiss* whoever made this!"

"I mean, if you insist," she said with an impish wink.

The roots of Abran's hair burned with embarrassment. "You...*you* made this?"

Calla reeled back with mock hurt. "Don't act so surprised! You might hurt my feelings."

Abran took another bite of the tart and decided to keep his fat mouth shut.

Calla kept bringing tarts. Her visits grew more frequent, to the point where she was in Abran's shop at least every other day, if not more, hiding until Inula left and then emerging to spend the rest of the day with Abran. Abran had had to let his belt out one size to accommodate all the tarts she had stuffed into him, but he didn't mind. He caught himself watching the door throughout the day, waiting for her to show up. Sometimes, once Inula had gone, Calla would emerge and help Abran arrange the displays, or would take it upon herself to tout the merits of a certain piece to customers. Abran's sales soared whenever she was in the store.

"I'm never going to keep up with demand the way you're selling things," he half-heartedly groused to her after one such encounter.

She just smiled and tossed her long, chestnut tresses over her shoulder. "Honestly, you ought to just make me a full partner at this point."

Abran liked the idea more than he probably should have.

Of all the days Calla came, though, Abran's favorites were when business was slow and he could close the shop early. They'd close all the doors and windows, spread the counter cloth over the floor, and just sit and talk while they had a strawberry tart picnic. Calla told Abran about growing up in the Golden Grove—about the trees that changed color depending on the time of day, the Sacred Flame that kept the Grove safe from the Woods of Desolation, and the unicorns that chose to bond with certain elves. She talked about her niece, Ash, but veered far away from conversations about Inula. In turn, Abran told her about growing up in Alvernet, about his family, the shop, and anything else she wanted to know. There was something about her that elicited the deepest of conversations. It was one of the many things he admired about her. He hoped their conversations, and the vibrancy she brought with her, never ended.

One day, though, Abran hardly noticed Calla come in. He had taken to leaving the cloth over the counter, and was stocking shelves when he noticed the cloth lift up and fall back into place—the flash of a boot heel disappear beneath it. Abran furrowed his brow. That wasn't like Calla. He moved to the counter to see what was wrong, but then a long shadow cast itself from the shop doorway.

Abran rounded on the figure. It had taken him weeks, but he had finally worked out what he planned to say to her the next time she entered his shop—to demand that she stop harassing Calla and just leave her in peace. But it was not Inula in the doorway. It was an elven man that Abran could only think to describe as beautiful. Tall and lean, his head brushed the top of the doorway, his porcelain skin nearly giving off a soft glow in the fading sunlight. His cheeks and jawline were soft and his long, light brown tresses silky. Everything about him belied gentleness and beauty and made Abran keenly aware of his rough hands, stubble, and odor that always smelled vaguely of tanning leather.

Abran was about to welcome the elf in as he would any other customer, but then he caught sight of the look in the elf's eyes. Sharp, hard, and *invasive*—scanning Abran's shelves like a hawk looking for a mouse.

Adrenaline scorched through Abran's veins. Something was not right. He moved to the doorway, barring access to the shop and, more importantly, to Calla. He folded his arms across his chest and looked up to meet the elf's eyes. "Something I can help you with?"

"I'm looking for someone," the elf said, his voice soft and smooth. He smiled—an expression that never reached his eyes. "I know this is a terrible inconvenience, but would you mind terribly if I looked around your shop for them? I could have sworn I saw them come in here."

Wary unease crept through Abran's stomach. "I would mind,

actually," he said, unblinking. "I won't have anyone disturb my customers."

The elf looked past Abran to the shop interior, which was empty. "But there's no one here."

"Ah, so you and I are in agreement, then. Whoever you're looking for's not here." Abran went to close the door, but the elf's hand shot out and caught the edge of it, finger's curling around the wood until his knuckles turned white. The door came to a dead stop.

"There's been a misunderstanding," he said, his voice as mild as icicles hurling through a winter storm. "I'd like to clear it up."

Abran looked up into the elf's face, which hadn't changed from its placid neutrality, but now it somehow looked twisted and feral. Cold, unfeeling, and guilty. Fury burned through Abran's fingertips and bristled along his shoulder and spine. This elf had done something to Calla. Of that, he had no doubt.

"*I'll* make something *very clear*," Abran said, his words dark with anger, even as a chill of trepidation raced down his spine. This was an *elf*. *Why* was he antagonizing someone that could turn him to dust with a look? But the words fell from his mouth, powerful and firm. "Any business you have here ends on this doorstep."

The elf sized Abran up as if determining if it would be worth it to push the subject. He curled his lip, his face twisting into something just as foul as what shone through his eyes. "I don't know what you think you're doing," he hissed. "But I assure you it will never be enough. The Ancient Races have no thought or care for the likes of you, and we never will."

"Oh no," Abran said, his tone flat and emotionless. "I am so hurt by your words. How ever shall I go on?"

The elf's prim nostrils flared. He released the door and swept away, his hair flicking in Abran's face and smelling of rotting flowers.

Abran shut and bolted the door after him, but even that didn't feel secure enough. He felt the elf's eyes boring through the windows, so he shuttered and locked those as well. He stuck old rags in any crevices big enough for someone to peek through, and jammed a chair against the door handle for extra measure. When he was satisfied that everything was fully secure, he sat himself in the farthest corner of the room away from the counter, giving Calla all the space she needed.

"Calla," he said softly. "You can come out, if you like. He's gone, and he's not getting in. If you want to leave, you can go through the passage behind the shelves in the back room. There's a series of marked tunnels there, and one will lead you right outside Alvernet. The key's on the shelf with the leather scraps." He took a breath, trying to slow the words down as they tumbled out of his mouth. "I'm in the corner and won't say anything to you if you don't want me to. Whatever you need."

No sound came from beneath the cloth. Abran wanted to say something more—to ask if she was all right or needed food or to just offer her some words of comfort—but he knew none of that would be helpful to *her* right now. It would just make him feel better. So, he waited.

The setting sun snuck in through the window cracks Abran couldn't cover and painted the walls in thin strokes of burnished copper. Those slid up the wall until they vanished and a cool, wet breeze slipped in around the door frame instead. Abran lit a candle. Rain pattered outside. And still Calla said nothing.

The candle had lost a third of its wax when the cloth finally shifted. Calla unfolded herself from beneath the counter, wrapped the cloth around her shoulders, and padded across the room. She didn't look Abran in the eyes, but she sat next to him and rested her head on his shoulder. Abran could almost feel the weight of her anguish in that one gesture. He rested his head against hers and closed his eyes, wishing he could take all that hurt away from her.

"He ate your strawberry tart," she said, so quietly it was almost a whisper.

Abran didn't care, but he could tell Calla did. So he let out an expletive that would have made his mother blush.

Calla nodded. "I was on my way over here when Inula showed up with him. She said I must have made the tart for him, then sat us down, made introductions, and left us alone." She shifted, her hands twisting the corner of the cloth. "I watched him eat all of it. I—I couldn't say anything. When he finally finished, I stood up and told him I had no interest in seeing him, and that Inula had orchestrated the whole thing. I went to leave, and then he, *he...*" Her lip quivered, and she sat up. She lifted the hem of her tunic to reveal deep red bruises along her hip—nearly perfect fingerprints.

Raging, inarticulate fury burned so brightly in Abran he saw stars in his eyes. It took every ounce of willpower in him not to break his own door down and charge after the elf that had dared to lay his hands on Calla.

"I've *never* had someone grab me—*hurt* me—like that," Calla whispered. "My mind went blank. I wrenched myself away and just left. I had no idea where I was going. I didn't even know he followed me until he was at the door, and—" She shook her head, and tears started to fall down her cheeks. She bit her lip and let out an angry sob. "I'm sorry. I'm sorry to cause you so much trouble. I'm sorry Inula is...Inula. And I'm sorry about the stupid strawberry tart." She half-laughed, half-sobbed, and buried her face in the counter cloth. Abran wrapped his arms around her and just held her, limbs shaking. There was nothing he could say or do to make her hurt go away, and that knowledge ate away at him.

Eventually, Calla's cries quieted, and her breathing deepened. Abran craned his neck to look at her, and found her eyelids fluttering, fighting with all their might to stay open and failing miserably. Her eyes were exhausted and unfocused.

Abran brushed the back of one of his knuckles over her cheek, clearing away some of the silvery tears. Her eyes refocused and she looked at him.

"I know you need to sleep," he said gently. "But a dusty shop floor is not the place to do that."

Her eyes widened with dread. "I can't go back to—"

Abran held up a hand to stave her off. "My family has an extra room with a bed in it." *His* bed, but he was happy to give it up for as long as she needed.

Her eyes filled with tears again, but, blessedly, they didn't fall. "I would like that," she said hoarsely. "Thank you, Abran."

Abran didn't know what it was about the way Calla said his name, but the sound roared like fire through his veins. He cleared his throat and untangled himself from her, helping her to her feet. "My grandfather was...odd. He didn't like interacting much with people outside of his shop, so he built tunnels to get him where he needed to go. Home, outside Alvernet, the outhouse..."

Calla chuckled faintly—only a shadow of her usual laugh, but still something. "Is there any way we could extend those tunnels to the Golden Grove?"

"I'm sure there'd be much better places you could spend time digging tunnels to than an old tanning and leather shop."

"But no other places with *you* in them," she remarked faintly.

The heat in Abran's cheeks spread to the tips of his ears and down his neck. He cleared his throat and ushered her to the back room. Grabbing the key off the scrap shelf, he swung a shelf away from the wall to reveal a tiny hidden passage. He lit the small lantern they kept at the entrance and took it off its hook, gesturing Calla into the passage after him. They walked through the narrow tunnel in complete silence save for the sound of the lantern guttering in Abran's hand.

They reached a round room with several tunnels shooting out in different directions from it, each labeled with a plank of wood. Abran led Calla through the "Home" tunnel, and they reached the trapdoor at the end of the passage without incident. Abran inched the door open and peeked inside. The house was dark save for the single candle his mother left for him anytime he was out late. Nothing else in the house stirred.

Abran blew out the lantern, hung it on the peg below the trapdoor, and then clambered out of the hole, helping Calla out after him. She let her gaze rove about the living area, her eyes getting some of their twinkle back. "It feels...nice in here. Like a home should feel." Her shoulders hunched, and she hugged her elbows tight to her sides. "Safe."

Abran had to work to keep his face neutral. If he ever saw that elf again...

He cleared his throat again to banish the violent thoughts rising to the surface of his mind. "The room is upstairs. Do you want me to show you to it now? Or make you some tea? Or..." He trailed off, realizing he may overwhelm her if he offered too many options.

Calla blinked wearily at him. "Sleep, I think. But tea in the morning?"

"Absolutely." Abran guided her to the single room upstairs, made sure she had enough blankets to keep herself comfortable, and then made his way back down to the main floor. He put his mother's table and chairs on top of the trap door and locked it in place before dragging a spare bed pallet in front of the front door. He didn't think there was any way someone could have followed them here, but he wasn't taking any chances.

He went to bed, dreaming of crumbled, spoiled strawberry tarts.

"Abran, are you *drunk*?"

Abran started awake to find his twelve-year-old sister standing over him, arms folded sternly.

Abran groaned and tried to judge the time by the light from outside. *Whatever* time it was, it was too early. "I'm not drunk, Isla."

She wrinkled her nose. "You *stink* like you're drunk. And you never put a pallet out unless you're too tipsy to walk up the stairs."

"I'll have you know I went up *and* down those stairs last night just fine," Abran retorted, snagging his sister and hooking her under his arm to tickle her. "I was just helping a friend out."

Isla shrieked indignantly and tried to wriggle away from his tickles, unsuccessfully masking her giggles. "Then they must be drunk, too!"

"I would like to note that I hold my liquor very well. I rarely get drunk."

Abran and Isla froze to look at Calla sitting on the stairs, watching them with amusement.

Isla let out a small gasp and looked at Abran with a scathing eyebrow. "How did *you* become friends with someone so pretty?"

Abran glanced at his sister, and then at Calla with a wry smile. "You know, that's something I never got to ask."

Calla leaned her chin in her palm, some of the familiar twinkle returning to her eyes as she looked at Abran. "Who says *you're* not pretty?"

Isla grimaced. "*I* do."

Before Abran could retaliate against Isla or try to explain away the blush creeping up his neck, his mother appeared from her bedroom in a tattered night dress. She looked blearily at her children. "I have always loved that you two get along, but could you perhaps keep it down until—" Her gaze slid up the stairs to Calla. Her face turned an alarming shade of purple as her eyes went wide with horror. "Abran Tanner!" she roared, clutching her night dress about her like shield. "Why do you *never* tell me when guests are coming?"

"When have I ever brought guests—"

Before Abran could finish, his mother had whirled and slammed her bedroom door behind her. "Pull out the bacon and cheese!" she barked as it sounded like she upended her entire bedroom behind the door. "And Abran, you are no son of mine if you haven't offered that woman something to drink!"

"He's already offered me tea!" Calla called helpfully, her eyes bright with amusement.

Abran mouthed a silent thank you.

"Well, there's hope for him yet," his mother muttered behind her door.

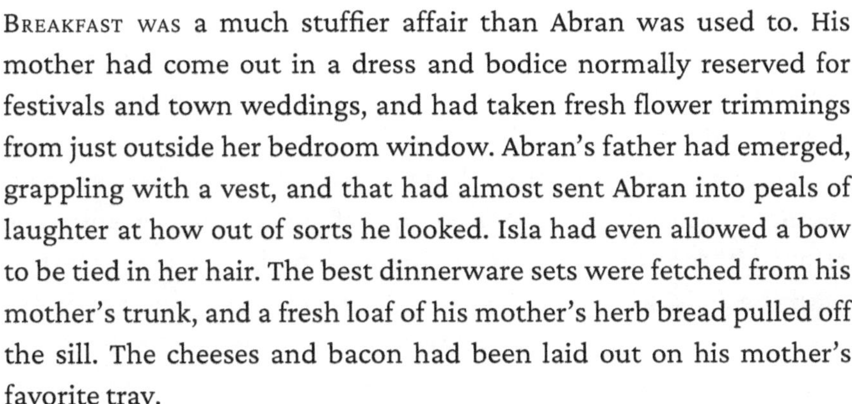

BREAKFAST WAS a much stuffier affair than Abran was used to. His mother had come out in a dress and bodice normally reserved for festivals and town weddings, and had taken fresh flower trimmings from just outside her bedroom window. Abran's father had emerged, grappling with a vest, and that had almost sent Abran into peals of laughter at how out of sorts he looked. Isla had even allowed a bow to be tied in her hair. The best dinnerware sets were fetched from his mother's trunk, and a fresh loaf of his mother's herb bread pulled off the sill. The cheeses and bacon had been laid out on his mother's favorite tray.

Calla took it all in graciously, but Abran saw some of her far-off hollowness returning. Abran's heart sank in his chest. He gently touched his mother's knuckles. When she looked at him, he flicked his eyes and tilted his head toward Calla. His mother followed his gaze. When she took in the way Calla clutched her tea cup in both hands, and the way her shoulders huddled ever so slightly over it, his mother's face softened in concern.

"Isla, the animals need tending. You've put off your chores long enough this morning."

Isla sighed. "Yes, ma." She untied the ribbon from her hair and tromped outside.

Abran's mother shooed her husband out the door as well, claiming there were urgent errands to be run in town. Despite his grumbling, Abran's father followed his wife willingly. They shared a kiss on the front stoop before closing the door behind them.

When they were alone in the house, Abran felt Calla's quiet darkness return. She stared at her knuckles and the tea going cold in her hands. Abran was reminded of a candle at the end of its wick, still bright, but threatening to blow out at any moment. Abran didn't know what to say, so he just sat with her in the silence, his gut clenched so tightly he couldn't bring himself to drink his own tea.

Calla tucked her knees close to her chest, her expression still vacant and far away. "When I was younger, Inula would comb my hair when I had a bad day," she said in almost a whisper.

"Do you...want me to comb your hair?" Abran asked gently.

Calla looked at him in wide-eyed surprise, and looked like she would turn down the offer. But then her lower lip trembled, and her eyes turned misty. "I would love that."

Abran helped her up from the table and set a pillow in front of his mother's arm chair. He located one of his mother's combs and cleaned it, and once it was dry, he settled into the arm chair. Starting with the ends, he piled Calla's long hair into his lap and pulled the comb through it. Abran had always expected elves to smell like the forest or flowers, but Calla just smelled...normal. The same as any other person he knew.

And she could get hurt like one, too.

Abran's hand clenched tighter around the comb as he thought of the dark fingerprints on Calla's hips. "Do you need help tending your injuries?"

Calla stiffened. Her hand drifted to her waist. "They're just bruises. I'll be fine."

"Did he hurt you anywhere else?" he asked carefully. He knew what the world was like for women. He had hoped it might be different for elves.

Calla shook her head slowly. "No," she said. "That doesn't mean he didn't want to, though." A shudder ran through her. She leaned back until her head rested on Abran's knee and let out a long, heavy sigh. "It's so quiet here," she said.

Abran snorted. "Did you and I have the same breakfast?"

"Not that way," she said, her eyes still closed. "It's more a...quiet of the heart, I suppose. You don't worry about how to act or what to say or how your family perceives you. You have the space to just *be*." There was a heart-wrenching sadness in her voice. "Home used to be that way, but now..."

"Calla, you can stay here as long as you like," Abran blurted, a surge of protectiveness swelling in his chest. "You can stay here until things get quiet back home. Or...or even longer, if you wanted."

Calla cracked one eye open, a hint or the normal mischievous gleam in her gaze. But, underneath it, Abran saw the deep resonance of relief and gratitude. "Careful," she rasped. "I might just think you have permanent intentions toward me."

Isla burst in at that moment, laden with fresh wild flowers, followed closely by Abran's parents. He and Calla were swept up into the activity, but as they laughed with his family, Abran's eyes kept straying to Calla, his thoughts dwelling on her mention of marriage. And how much he liked the idea.

ABRAN STROLLED BACK to the tannery that night, his brow furrowed in contemplation. He whistled aimlessly to himself—more as a distraction from thoughts of Calla than anything else. Not that it did much good. What was he *doing*? Had he truly fallen for—? And had *she*—?

"You would almost be adorable if you weren't so pathetic." Inula peeled herself from the shadows cast by a nearby lantern, her flaxen hair glittering like cobwebs.

Abran stopped and folded his arms against his chest, protecting the happiness there. "I didn't expect to see you here," he said, barely masking his anger.

"I'm sure you didn't," Inula said with a sneer. Abran couldn't understand how two sisters could be so unalike. Inula rested her form languidly against a stall, arms folded and long fingers tapping against her bicep. "I hope you don't have any intentions toward my sister."

"If I did," Abran said, straightening his shoulders, "I hope she would be permitted to make her *own* choice on the matter."

Inula laughed—a tinkling of chimes just barely off-key. "What *choice* is there to make? You are a *child* to her. She has already lived several of your lifetimes, and will live many more after you are nothing but worm food in the ground. What sort of existence would that be for either of you?"

Abran curled his fingers tighter around his arms, his anger building to fury. "A better choice than the men *you* bring around. The last one *hurt* her. When are you going to stop with this insane parade of suitors?"

Inula went quiet, her body rigid. There was a flash of pain across her face. "I can assure you, Hawthorn was dealt with. He won't be hurting anyone again." The light in her eyes was deadly. Abran was glad to see they at least agreed on how that elf should have been dealt with. "How is she?" Inula asked quietly.

"Not well!" Abran snapped. "She's safe now, but how long will that stay the case when she's under your care? Are you going to keep bringing these suitors around that she plainly has no interest in?"

"Interest doesn't matter!" Inula crossed the space between them, her face furious. "What matters is that she has someone to take care of her after I can't be there anymore!"

Abran didn't back down. He just leveled a disgusted look at her. "Of course interest matters. What is life without someone you care about to share it with?" He ground his teeth. "Have you ever loved *anyone*, Inula?"

She curled her lip. "I thought I had, once, when I was young and stupid and hadn't yet learned that *feelings* aren't the cure to everything. Another mixed union gone wrong."

Abran reared back. He hadn't expected *Inula*, of anyone, to have loved someone other than an elf. He shook his head. It didn't matter what her past was. Her bitterness was still trying to control him and, worst of all, her own sister.

"I would rather live one day with true love than a thousand life-times without it," he said.

"But will *she*?" Inula's eyes burned like twin flames in the dark.

Abran drew himself up, head thrown back. "At least she'd still be able to make a *choice*, rather than you taking it away from her."

"And what makes you think I don't already know her answer?" Inula drew herself up to her full, threatening height. "She is my *sister*. I know every secret, every wish, every longing of her heart. Over two-hundred years of memories, and you come to me thinking you know more about her in a matter of *months*?"

"Then explain why she came to *me* when she needed help," Abran shot back, unable to keep the fury out of his voice any longer.

Inula loomed over him now, her face contorted in a snarl. Her eyes flashed with murderous light. "I tried to warn you away gently, but you leave me no choice but to shatter your misplaced infatua-tion," she said, the words hissing through clenched teeth. "She *will* be betrothed to another—an elf that will take far better care of her than you ever will. So, I suggest you find a nice human woman to lust after so you two can live out the rest of your miserable lives together. Calla is destined for greater things than you."

She swept off into the night, leaving Abran feeling as if all the breath had been sucked from his lungs.

WHEN ABRAN GOT HOME that night, Calla wasn't there. She had left a note with his parents, saying that she needed to sort some things at home, but that she would be back in a day. She had taken the counter cloth with her. Abran tried not to let Inula's words repeat in his mind. Calla would be back. He knew she would.

He excused himself to bed early, feeling strange and out of place going to his own bedroom. He laid in the bed, hoping it might still have some of her warmth. It did not.

He buried himself deeper in the blanket. It was fine. He was over-reacting. Calla would be back tomorrow, and then the inexplicable hole in his heart would be filled. He went to sleep.

But Calla didn't return the next day.

Or the day after that.

Or the day after *that.*

Abran couldn't sit still. He wandered through his home and his shop as if a saber were chasing him. The shop had never looked so spotless—the shelves never more organized. *Anything* to keep the truth from catching up to him. He carried Calla's letter with him at all times, reading her promise that she would be back over and over again. Inula's words floated about his shoulder like an obnoxious crow.

Calla is destined for greater things than you.

It was five days when Abran's lack of rest and manic working finally caught up to him. He sat in the back room, his hands frozen over a piece of hide he had been shaving. His eyes went wide, and the tool dropped out of his hands. He hunched over and buried his face in his palms as the weight of the truth plowed into him like a battering ram. She wasn't coming back. Calla wasn't coming back. The knowledge settled so fully on his shoulders that it felt as if it would break his spine.

Abran heard the shop door open.

"We're closed!" he called gruffly, not moving from where he sat.

The new customer didn't seem to care. Their footsteps tromped heavy and loud against the wooden floor—quickly approaching the back room.

Abran growled, every nerve in him alighting with anger. "I *said* we're—" He looked up, and the words died in his throat. There, in his doorway, was none other than Inula, her eyes wide and enraged. And fearful.

She flung her hand at Abran, her green eyes glowing, and he flew back against the wall as branches sprouted from the wood and lashed him into place.

"Where is she?" Inula roared. "What have you done with her?"

It took a moment for Abran's spinning, throbbing head to pick up on what she meant. When it did, though, his body stilled and his heart skipped a beat. Calla. She was looking for Calla.

Which meant Calla had never made it home.

Abran's face turned white.

"Finally afraid now that you've been caught?" Inula snarled.

"Are you telling me you waited a *week* before looking for her?" Abran screamed at her. The outrage coursed like an extra surge of strength through his veins. He strained his arms and broke free of Inula's bindings, which crumbled around him. The moment he was free, he ran past Inula, wrenching haphazard pieces of protective equipment off his shelves and strapping it on.

Inula followed him. "You are *not* getting out of this so—"

"She's not here!" Abran roared. He brandished Calla's letter at Inula. She snatched it from him, and her eyes grew wide as she read it, her fingers trembling. Abran drew a knife from his workshop, and a bow and arrow as well. His eccentric grandfather had always like to be prepared in case of emergencies. Abran's heart beat against his ribs in a thundering panic. All he saw were Hawthorn's hollow, cruel eyes as he had tried to force his way into the shop—the bruises on Calla's hips.

"Where are *you* going?" Inula asked him, her voice sounding small and shaken.

"To do the job you can't seem to do," he snapped. "You want to tell me where she is, since you know her 'every secret and every wish'?"

Inula looked like she had been slapped. She still straightened, though. "I'm coming with you."

"No, you're not." He cinched up his straps, not deigning to look at her. "You've done enough already. I'm going to find her, and make sure she's safe. It that monster, Hawthorn, touched her again, I'm going to kill him. I have much less patience for abuse than you seem to." He left Inula there, not caring what she did after that. All that mattered was Calla.

Abran's mind raced with fear as he ran down the main square of Alvernet, his leather pieces jangling around on him. Calla was all alone. He should have stopped being sorry for himself *days* ago and gone looking for her. He should have chased after her the minute she left. Then she wouldn't be in danger—wouldn't have fallen victim to Hawthorn all over again. Abran would never forgive himself for that. He was prepared to take on the whole Golden Grove on his own if it meant getting her back. If it meant that she would get to smile again and feel safe. He clenched and unclenched the knife at his side and adjusted the bow better on his shoulder. He would go to war for her.

The people and houses blurred past him until he was in the rolling countryside, churning up dust in his wake as he ran. Every footstep—every heartbeat—thudded with her name. Calla, Calla, *Calla.*

A tall, lithe figure emerged from the Woods of Desolation, carrying a lantern in one hand and something white tucked against their chest. Abran almost didn't register them until he saw the long, chestnut hair.

He came to an immediate stop, his chest heaving. He rubbed at his eyes—had he just imagined it? Simply manifested a mirage of what he wanted to see most? But when he opened his eyes again, she was still there—striding toward him with the most beautiful smile Abran had ever seen.

Calla stopped short a few meters from Abran, her head tilting to one side and her brow furrowing with a question. "Is this a new service you're offering?" she asked. "Wearing in your pieces for your clients so they don't have to?"

Abran's knees trembled, threatening to give way at any moment. "Are you hurt?" he asked, his voice rasping in his throat.

Calla's smile faded. "Why would I be hurt?"

"Calla, please," he said, not able too look at her. He passed his hand across his face. "Just answer the question."

"I'm not hurt, I promise. Abran, what is—"

Abran sat down hard in the dirt, legs bent, arms dangling over his knees, and head bowed. He took several long, calming breaths, banishing the scenarios that had raced through his mind where he had to obliterate an entire elven community to save Calla. His heartbeat pounded somewhere in his throat.

"Abran!" Calla crouched next to him, hovering nervously. "What did I do? Are *you* all right? Can I do something? What do you—?"

Without looking up, Abran just grabbed one of her hands, squeezing it. Calla went silent, and they sat that way for a long time. The sun rose overhead, and birds whistled in the tall, soughing grasses. It took Abran's hands a long time to stop trembling. She was *there*. Calla was *safe*. So why did he still feel so terrified?

"Abran," she said gently. "Look at me, please."

He did. When his eyes met her lily-green ones—so bright they almost glowed—it felt as if his mouth filled with sawdust.

"What did I do to scare you?" she asked.

Abran swallowed hard. He kissed her knuckles, and pink spread across her nose. "I thought you weren't coming back," he whispered.

Calla took in the armor he had donned. He imagined he looked fairly ridiculous with the haphazard pieces all cobbled together. "Were you coming to...save me?" she asked, her voice warm.

"I was," he said miserably. "If it was something or someone keeping you from coming back, I would have torn the whole world apart. But I..." He couldn't look her in the eyes. "I was afraid that you were *choosing* not to come back. Inula had said...And I don't know how I—"

He looked up at her just as she grabbed both sides of his face and kissed him.

Abran's spine stiffened. His eyes went wide, and all the color left his face. He tried to pull away, shocked, but she just gripped him tighter. "I love you, Abran Tanner," she said against his lips. "And don't you *dare* listen to a thing my sister says ever again." She pulled away from him then, her eyes brimming with tears. And she looked *angry.* "*You* are my choice. The man that makes me laugh—the man that makes me feel safe and protected and welcomes me into his space. The man that puts on ridiculous armor to come save me even when he's wildly outmatched." She took his hand again. "You are brave and smart and *good* and everything I wish I could be. You are Abran Tanner, and I *choose. You.*"

Calla handed him the white bundle she had been carrying. He looked at it, and his jaw dropped open when he realized what it was. It was the counter cloth, washed until it gleamed and quilted to another soft fabric lining. In the corner, two letters had been embroidered in gold. C and A.

"I went back to the Golden Grove to collect some things. There's a healer named Hemlock that helps to hide me from Inula. I really was going to be gone just a day, but, I did this instead." Calla traced her fingers over the letters. "I was going to put an A as a thank you, but as I kept working the C just...appeared." She fidgeted, looking suddenly uncomfortable. "I hope you don't mind. I probably should have—"

It was Abran's turn to kiss her. He wrapped his arms around her waist and pulled her into his lap. Her warmth seared into him, melding them to each other. He took in her scent—her normal, average scent that made his head spin. How? How had he gotten someone so perfect to love him? He pressed his lips to hers, sunlight pouring into him from the touch. His hand rested on the gentle curve of her neck. Her hand brushed his cheek. Abran had never felt so happy—so *right.* "Careful," he rasped against her lips. "I might just think you have permanent intentions toward me."

She smiled. "Then I'm doing a good job."

CREED OF THE LIGHT CHASERS

When pillars descend
From silver clouds
And burnish the land in gold
To this treasure I must go
And learn the secrets of the gods.
No Man nor beast nor mortal life
Shall stay my fated course
No life I'd rather lead than this.
For I am a chaser of light.

THE DAY OF BLUEST BLOOD

Monterro's streets blazed with life and color. Every cobblestone unclaimed by brick and mortar buildings had been turned over to stalls, street vendors, and performers. Steam simmered from glistening meat, jigs and reels called to each other from across the way, and Loralan's pendants of blue, purple, and gold streamed from every available roof and window. And still people managed to squeeze between them all.

Gan gripped Merra's hand tighter in his and dodged through the crowd. He supposed that, for once, he should be grateful Sister Earth blessed him with small shoulders and a narrow frame.

"You would think the novelty of the queen's pregnancy would wear off after the last five!" Gan's wife chuckled breathlessly, brushing her crown of copper curls from her face. Her smile was bright and mostly genuine, but ten years of marriage had taught Gan to notice the tautness between her cheeks and eyes; the invisible scars of the wounds left behind by her tears.

Gan squeezed her hand and plucked a red pea blossom from one of the trellises splashed about the square. "I'm thrilled for any party I get to enjoy with you," he said with a bow as he folded the flower into Merra's hand.

The tightness vanished from her face, and she wreathed him in her breathtaking, crooked smile. "And I you." She affixed the red blossom to her hair and pulled him through the crowd. "But we can enjoy ourselves later. We can't have you missing the Council Meeting!"

"Perhaps I should bring some masks along with me," Gan said as he glanced at the festive things festooned with ribbons and feathers in every color imaginable.

"I doubt that would cure Lord Alvace of his poor temper."

"No, but it would certainly do wonders for mine." The mask cart trundled off into the crowd. "Do you think his breath would make the ribbons curl?"

She laughed outright, the sound trilling away across the crowd.

The trek to the castle gates was arduous at worst, and an adventure at best. The fanfare and hubbub was infectious, leaving both Gan and Merra feeling like children again. He snuck kisses whenever he could, and she giggled and scrunched her nose each time.

When they reached the castle gates, the guards nodded to them and ushered them to the royal family's private courtyard.

Queen Eden waited for them there, dressed simply with a sparse gold band twisted into her equally golden hair, but resplendent in the glowing smile she gave her children as they tumbled over each other. She rested a dainty hand on her belly, only barely beginning to swell. Her oldest—a broad-shouldered sixteen-year-old every bit the image of his father—stood sentinel over his sisters and brothers, the picture of grim dignity. But every so often, the sun caught a sparkle in his eye and a smile at the corner of his mouth. Glimpses of his mother. The sight gave Gan hope for the future of the kingdom.

Merra pulled up short at the sight, her hand tight in Gan's. "She was *made* to be a mother, wasn't she?" she asked, her voice low, breathless, and longing.

Gan pulled her to his side and leaned his head on hers.

"Do you think, if things had been different and you were a noble-man, you would have married her?" she asked.

Gan stroked her hair. "Perhaps. We had been friends long enough that I wouldn't see why not. Salaith would have fought for her, though. For all his flaws, at least he loves her fiercely." Gan touched her chin and turned her face towards him. Her green eyes swam with the memory of the orchard where they had met so many years ago. "And besides, if things were different, I would have never met you." He kissed her long and deep until her face turned as red as the roots of her hair. "And I would be a very sorry man without you in my life."

She chuckled and brushed a curl away from her face, batting her long lashes at him.

"Gan!" Four-year-old Prince Ro bustled over to them, chubby hands laden with earthworms. "Look!" He shoved the worms closer.

His wife kissed the skin just above Gan's collar, sending a shock of giddiness through him, before she crouched to Ro's height.

"Thank you! These will be perfect in my garden!" She helped Ro carefully arrange the worms in her apron.

Gan cleared his throat, pulled at his collar to let some steam escape, and bent to help them.

"Ro, why don't you go with Ilys and Elem to see if your butterflies have hatched?" Queen Eden approached, mouthing a silent apology to Gan's wife for her ruined apron.

Ro set his mouth defiantly. "But, Gan shows me all the *big* bugs!"

Gan jumped at the raised eyebrows from both women. "Shhh!" he hissed out of the corner of his mouth to Ro. "That's *our* secret, remember?"

Ro put his hands over his mouth, eyes wide. "Did I get in trouble?"

"No, but I think *I* did." Gan stood with a barely suppressed groan and shooed Ro along after his older sisters.

"These bugs wouldn't happen to be in the game forest, would they?" Eden asked, perfectly poised and dangerous.

"They're *certainly* not from the medicine bogs I've told you to stay away from on more than one occasion." His wife said in an equally warning voice.

Gan quailed beneath their stares. He had to remember to find new spots for the prince's bug foraging. He cleared his throat. "Your Highness, I do believe we have a council meeting to attend?"

A smile quirked at Eden's mouth. "Ever the diplomat, aren't you?" She turned to Gan's wife. "Do you mind horribly if I steal him from you for a few hours? I promise to have him back in plenty of time for you to enjoy the festival at your leisure."

Merra curtsied. "Have him for as long as you like, your Highness. He is ever so much more obedient after being beneath your excellent tutelage."

The women shared a look and laughed as Gan spluttered.

"Also, congratulations, your Highness," Merra said, her voice wistful. "May the child lead a blessed and happy life."

Eden took her hand in both of hers. "Thank you. Would to Sister Earth I could spread my blessing to you, my dear friend."

Merra bowed, her eyes misty. "Thank you." She dabbed at her eyes and cleared her throat. "Now, if I may, I think I'll supervise the butterflies as well." She kissed Gan on the cheek and followed the path of mud and loose hair ribbons to the children.

Eden watched her go. "Should anything happen to me, I hope you know I would send my children to you in a heartbeat."

"We would be honored." Gan watched his wife disappear around a bend, spine straight, hair billowing out behind her in a crimson blaze. He would never know how he had managed to woo such a strong, fierce woman. "I hope it never comes to that, but should it, you know she would treat them as her own."

Eden bumped his shoulder. "As would you, I would hope." She turned toward the Council Room and Gan followed after her. "How prepared are you for this meeting?"

"As ready as I ever am for Lord Alvace to flay me with words he barely understands."

Eden covered her mouth and coughed delicately, as close as she could get to a laugh at the expense of the minister without appearing unduly biased. Gan missed the days they laughed at nonsense until they choked on tears. "Is there anything you needed me to have prepared for this meeting?" he asked.

She was silent for longer than he had anticipated. She absently rubbed her belly and watched the pennants streaming from the white spires of Castle Monterro. "I do not begin to expect you to have a perfect knowledge of things, although I know you try," she said with a sideways look and a half smile. The smile vanished quickly, though. "But I do know that you are more in tune with my people than the men that sequester themselves behind stone walls. And, regrettably, more in tune than I am. In your honest opinion, how do you feel the state of affairs are with the people? *My* people?"

Gan didn't know what to say. With the echoes of laughter, music, and general delight seeping through every crack from outside, the question seemed absurd at best. But he remembered the murmurings. The unease and cursory glances at the outskirts of the city. Rumors he had brushed aside as mere rumblings now became more vivid. More real. He looked at Eden with renewed respect. She had always had a way with knowing the heartbeats of those around her.

"I've heard whispers about Lord Tandiv's third son, Osmen. Nothing more than rumors, really, in the outer villages—"

Eden waved him off. "You know you don't need to justify your sources to me. Just tell me what you've heard."

Gan released a heavy sigh. He hated to be the bearer of unrest. "They say unsavory sorts have been flocking to Osmen in droves. Dismissed soldiers, fallen knights. Highwaymen and perhaps even a few warlocks. Crime has increased in the lower town over the past few months, and I doubt it's a coincidence."

"Oh, that we should be so fortunate." Eden pulled at her lip in thought, a habit that had survived from childhood. "Anything unusual or alarming in these crimes?"

"Nothing other than their influx." Gan scratched his jaw. "Although, I can't help but feel that a collection of that sort wouldn't congregate simply to rob inn-keepers of their nights' wages. I'm only sorry I didn't put the pieces together until now."

"I've had my suspicions about Osmen as well," Eden said, her expression darkening. "That boy has far too much ambition to be content with a portion of his father's estate. I should have had you keep an eye on it sooner."

"Is His Majesty aware of your concerns?"

Eden's hand tightened fractionally around her belly. "He has been caught up in his schemes for expansion deeper into the Phoenix Ridges. I've hardly seen him, much less had a moment to speak with him."

Gan couldn't respond to that. Nothing he could have said would have spared her feelings. Though Salaith was his king, Gan struggled to muster the appropriate respect for him. He tolerated him for Eden's sake, but the man was too prideful. Too bloodthirsty. He had gorged on his father's successes from the border disputes across the sea, and now peace was never enough. He had to have more land, more subjects, more power. For now, his schemes had been purely speculation, but Gan shuddered at the thought of what might happen the day they became something more. Right now, they coexisted rather easily with Golden Grove elves buried deep in Architect's Heart. But, if Salaith insisted on encroaching further into their territory to strip the mountain of its star crystals, there would be no telling when the elves would snap. Their memory was long, for both good and bad. Bloodshed would follow. And the fact that Salaith was ignoring his queen in favor of these war games made it all the more despicable.

Eden must have sensed his turmoil. She put a hand on his shoulder. "I know what you're thinking." She quelled a retort that filled Gan's lungs despite himself. "You have always been *terrible* at hiding your feelings."

Gan begrudgingly gave her the point.

"I know that you and my husband have never seen eye to eye on anything. You think he's too rigid. He thinks you're too soft. I know that the way he goes about things is abrasive and far more militant than either you or I would hope for, but he does it out of love for his people."

Gan raised an eyebrow in disbelief. Eden chuckled, warmth spreading to her cheeks. "When he and I are alone, you would be surprised how different he is. If it were up to him, we would live on an island far away with no responsibilities and only ourselves to worry about. He doesn't care for power and glory. But he does know that the crystals in Architect's Heart could eliminate hunger and poverty from the lower towns and smaller villages."

Gan bowed his head, sufficiently chastised.

Eden chuckled. "If you will promise to be gentle with him, I will promise to bring up all my concerns. We can be grateful for the fact that we have caught onto Osmen's machinations before they came to fruition."

Gan bowed. "Wise as ever, Your Highness."

She scoffed. "If I had the luxury of true wisdom, we wouldn't be in this mess, would we?"

They proceeded to the council room.

As an annex to the throne room, the sparse, low-ceilinged council room filled only with a long-table and twelve chairs paled in comparison to the vaulted ceiling, lavishly decorated columns, and candle-lit chandeliers in the throne room. Gan appreciated the simplicity, but the sight of the chamber always filled him with dread.

Gan took his seat at the foot of the table while Eden settled beside her husband at the head. The king immediately took his queen's hand in his. He did not acknowledge Gan, a very pointed gesture considering he greeted each of the other council members by name as they trickled into their seats. Gan still bowed anyway. He was used to the exchange. He had earned his seat, no matter what anyone else said, and he would act the part. The lords that sat on either side of Gan nodded and asked after his wife. He happily boasted of her garden while they nodded along, asking after her techniques. Gan had to remember that not all on the council were against him.

When all had taken their seats, a serving girl laden with goblets distributed them to the table, and the king called the council to commence.

"If at all possible," he said, stroking his beard, "I would like to make this brief so I may properly celebrate my queen."

All the members inadvertently cast glances at Lord Landwin, whose propensity for theatrics often lasted well into the night. He paled and sipped at his wine while clearing his throat. "Nothing to discuss here, sire. The ports are trading excellently, and we have seen neither hide nor hair of pirates since our last meeting. I believe the storms over the Shansay Seas have kept them at bay."

"Which will make them all the more desperate when they do come," Salaith said. "Ready your port guards and double their numbers, if you can. The storms may weaken the pirates, but wounded animals are more deadly than healthy ones."

Lord Landwin bowed his head. "It will be done, sire."

The rest of the meeting followed in a similar vein. The eastern villages had nearly been flooded out by angry naiads. Soldiers were dispatched to dig the villagers out and deliver aid. No one spoke a word of what happened to the naiads. Lord Fulnom had passed in his sleep, and the lordship had passed to his brother. The list of talking points ran long.

Gan took notes and listened as best he could, but his mind was on the men gathering at Osmen's side. What could their purpose be? Surely he didn't think to take his father's estate by force? But what else could it be?

He was so caught up in his thoughts that he missed the first time Salaith called his name, and started at the second time and nearly spilled his untouched wine. "My apologies, sire," he said as he dabbed droplets from his parchment. "I was lost in thought."

"Can't imagine over what. Not much to think about when you're playing Lady's Maid, is there?" Lord Alvace muttered to the Lord sitting next to him, just loud enough for Gan to hear. His pointed side-eye glance made it clear that had been intentional.

Gan cleared his throat. "The *queen*," he cast an equally pointed look back at Lord Alvace, "has assigned me to monitor the lower towns in Monterro. Over the past several months, the towns have seen a steady increase in petty crime."

"Not unusual for the lower sectors," Lord Landwin chimed in. "There has always been a higher risk of crime there."

"Yes. However, the increase we are seeing as of late is unusual. Reports have been—"

"It's because we allow them to propagate," Lord Alvace said, cutting Gan off—a favorite hobby of his. "We have wasted too much manpower and resources trying to build those sectors. Now that they are "safer", the felons can reproduce at their leisure. I say we remove our presence for a while and let the reprobates kill themselves off. That should help the crime rate significantly."

Gan was always somehow amazed at the pure vileness that could come out of Alvace's mouth. He always wondered how he had managed to secure himself a spot as a "servant to the people".

Eden straightened in her chair and folded her hands in her lap. To anyone that didn't know her, she was the picture of quiet poise. However, Gan had seen the anger in her eyes too many times to count. "Lord Alvace forgets that the revitalization of the lower towns is a project his queen founded and continues to have faith in," she said, each word perfectly enunciated and clipped. "All of our citizens deserve the safety and means to...propagate, as you say." She lifted one delicate eyebrow. "I believe the reason behind the increasing crime concerns will be revealed if we allow Counselor Gan to finish his report without interruptions."

Alvace's lips paled as he pressed them together. He bowed his head to Eden. "My queen."

Gan also nodded to Eden and continued. "The reports from the lower towns have indicated that highwaymen, rogue mercenaries, and the like have been gathering in increasing numbers to the lower towns."

Lord Alvace opened his mouth to speak again, but Eden quelled him with a look.

Gan continued, trying not to smile to himself. "While that in and of itself is concerning, there has also been mention of Osmen, Lord Tandiv's son, on more than one occasion with this lot. I fear that he may be planning something that does not bode well for Monterro."

Salaith sat in the silence that followed Gan's last statement, his expression hard and unreadable. "This is a grave accusation you bring to the table, counselor," he said, as unmoving as a rock. "Lord Tandiv has been a noble and loyal servant of this court for many years."

"I do not believe Lord Tandiv has any part to play in this. I do believe that his *son*, however—"

"To accuse a son is to accuse a father," Lord Alvace growled.

"I disagree," Gan said, taking a bracing breath against the Pit he was about to throw himself into. "Osmen is an adult and agent unto himself. Lord Tandiv has nothing to do with the concerns that—"

"And what *are* your concerns exactly, Counselor Gan?" Alvace asked, again cutting Gan off.

Gan glanced to Salaith, even though he knew he would receive no help on that front. He was not wrong. Eden's lips were pressed so tightly together that they nearly disappeared. She gave Gan a subtle nod—permission to approach the stupidity of the question as he saw fit.

"My *concerns*, Lord Alvace, are that we are ignoring very clear signs that a threat of some kind is building against our people."

Alvace scoffed. "And what *threat* does a ragtag group of thugs pose against the great palace of Monterro?"

Gan pinched the bridge of his nose. Surely someone with the finest resources and education at their disposal could not be so dense. And yet, Alvace always reveled in proving him wrong. "It is not the *palace* I am most concerned about. It is the people we have sworn to protect that are in the greatest danger."

"And as I said before, the lower towns can do with a little culling."

"Lord Alvace," Salaith warned. "Your queen has already made it clear that the lower towns have her full support and protection. That is not up for negotiation."

Lord Alvace flushed. Gan couldn't tell if it was from fear or rage, but either way he had to fight to keep a look of snotty triumph off his face. If Salaith was siding with him—even if in some small part— then there was very little for Alvace to do. Gan had won.

That didn't mean Alvace had to lose gracefully.

He narrowed his eyes at Gan, his entire face pinched and sour. "Are you certain, Counselor, that this has nothing to do with your distaste for His Majesty's bid toward expansion?"

Gan gave him a perplexed look. "That has nothing to do with the situation at hand."

"Are you certain? This is a threat that could easily be fabricated to draw our attention away from the objectives you so despise."

"Lord Alvace, you take this too far," Eden snapped. "Counselor Gan has been in my service since I was a girl. I trust him implicitly. He would never fabricate something for his own agenda."

"But, my queen, he has said himself that we cannot trust anyone, not even the sons of our most loyal allies."

"That is different, and you know it." Heat rose to Gan's face, burning holes in his diplomacy and tact.

"Then please, Counselor." Lord Alvace splayed his hands on the table. "Tell us what your ambitions are. What is your goal?"

"My goal is to protect the children of this kingdom from a future filled with unnecessary bloodshed!" Gan knew the moment the heated, shouted words left his mouth, he had lost. It didn't matter that it was the truth–that it was a noble goal. What mattered was his temper had gotten the better of him, and now, whatever else he said for the remaining meeting would be tainted by it.

But Architects forbid Alvace won on technicality alone.

"Then perhaps you should leave such matters to those who *have* children," he said with a smug grin.

The silence enveloped the room like a great monster snapping its jaws shut. Gan gaped at Lord Alvace, inarticulate from the fury raging through his ears.

Eden was the first to speak. She stood, her chair squealing against the stone floor. "Lord Alvace, you go too far!"

Gan rose with her, collecting his notes haphazardly, his vision stained red. "My king, my queen, I'm afraid I'll have to excuse myself from the rest of this meeting," he said with masterful control over his voice. "I worry great harm may befall Lord Alvace were I to stay a moment longer."

Eden tried to stop Gan with a placating hand, but he shook his head and brushed past her with a brief, clipped apology. Alvace laughed him all the way out of the room.

When he emerged, he nearly plowed through a servant carrying an empty tray—presumably to gather the empty goblets the lords had left on the table. She pirouetted out of his way, but tripped on her skirt. Someone caught her before she fell.

"Oh! Sir Osmen! Thank you!"

Gan called a hasty, haphazard apology, not fully seeing any of them. He stormed into the courtyard, fumes spilling from the heated words he muttered under his breath. How dare Alvace? How *dare* he? The snubs, the askance looks, the not-so-subtle whispers—he could handle all of them. But bringing Merra into the firing range? Alvace had gone too far, and Gan would not stand for it.

His one consolation was Eden speaking up for him, but he knew in the long run that would not be enough. The lords only saw her as a pretty trinket on Salaith's arm. It didn't matter the number of times she had risked herself for the kingdom, or how her presence alone had stalled more wars in their tracks than they could count. Changes had to be made, and they had to be made *now*, before Loralan found itself in complete upheaval.

After nearly half-an-hour of walking off his ire, Gan finally slowed his pace. He was not the only one that had been slighted in the council room. Eden had as well, and she had dealt with it with all the grace of her position. It didn't mean it hurt any less. She needed as much room to vent as he did at the moment. He smiled grimly to himself. At least they had each other to commiserate with. He turned on his heel and went to find her.

The deeper he came to the heart of the castle, though, the more a dark unease settled over him. He faltered in his steps, the hairs on the back of his neck rising. Something had gone quiet. Dark. He couldn't say why. Servants and soldiers alike still wandered through on their various daily errands. The general gaiety from outside still trickled through the walls. But something else was there. Eyes watching. Waiting. For what, he didn't know.

And then a scream pierced the courtyard.

A serving girl, tears streaming down her face, stumbled into the courtyard, heaving from a sprint. Gan recognized her as the girl that had brought the council their wine. "Someone! Someone help, please!" She tripped over a paving stone and fell to her knees but didn't seem to care. "They're dead! They're all dead!"

Gan ran to her as other onlookers were drawn to her screams. They hadn't seemed to have caught what she was saying, but were simply fascinated by a girl in hysterics. Gan took her by the shoulders as she bawled, her whole body seized and trembling in panic. "What's going on? *Who's* dead?"

She tried to wrench away from him as if he had assaulted her, but then she must have recognized him. Her eyes, scared and red-rimmed, widened. "Counselor Gan, how are you—? Why are you here? I saw you at the Council…"

Gan headed her off before she could slip into unimportant details. "I left the meeting early. What happened?"

Her lip trembled, and tears bubbled anew from her eyes as her face turned white. "The lords, sire…I went back to refill their goblets, and they…They were all dead. Folded over the table like sacks of flour. Their eyes…they just…they just stared."

Gan's blood fled from his face. The strength seeped from his limbs, and he felt as if he might faint. He bit the inside of his cheek and squeezed her harder, as much for his benefit to stay upright as for hers to stay focused. "Are you sure?"

Her lower lip trembled, and a shudder ran through her. "Sure as I'll ever be. I would never lie about something so horrible, sire, I can promise you."

"And the king and queen? Where are they?"

"Not there, sire. I'm not sure where they might be." She brought her hand to her mouth with a horrified gasp. "You don't think something horrible has happened to Her Majesty, do you? Not with her babe on the way!"

Gan shook his head as relief swept through him, but only for a moment. Just because Salaith and Eden weren't in the room with the council lords didn't mean they weren't in danger. He had to do something. A well and true crowd had gathered now, curious and oblivious, but that had to change. Now. There was a killer in the castle, and he had to get everyone mobilized before they could kill again.

The serving girl had taken to muttering, rocking back and forth as she held herself. "This is all like he said it would be. I didn't want to believe him, but he was right. Now they're dead. All dead, just like he said."

Gan's heart froze in his chest. He curled around the girl to shield her from the onlookers. "Just like who said?" he hissed.

The girl looked back at him. All reason had left her eyes. Her gaze darted wildly around the assembled people. "He said he saw the king put something in the council's drinks. I didn't believe him." She began to laugh, something throaty and feral. She tore at her hair and screamed at the crowd in hysterics. "King Salaith killed his council. Sir Osmen saw him do it!"

Osmen. The world tilted beneath Gan. It had never been about the lower towns. No. He had set his sights far higher.

More screams reverberated through the castle. Servants and townsfolk poured into the courtyard where Gan sat, their bodies covered in blood and bruises and their eyes wild. "The guards are attacking us! They turned their blades on the royal children!"

The serving girl screamed. "He's killed his council, and now he's turning on us!"

The crowd erupted and fled with screams and cries of horror. Gan's grip dropped from the serving girl. Cold sweat trickled down his spine. No. Salaith had done many things, but he would *never* hurt his... Gan surged to his feet. He rushed in the opposite direction of the crowd, an anguished sound wrenched from his throat. Not the children. Not *Merra*.

His feet couldn't move fast enough even as his mind thrashed itself to bits. *Why?* Why was Osmen doing this? *How* was he doing it? It didn't matter. Merra. *Merra.* She had to be all right. She *had* to be!

A guard lunged at Gan from the shadows, wordless and emotionless as he lurched forward, spear-tip aimed for Gan's heart. Gan tried to dodge out of the way, but it was a loose piece of cobblestone that saved him. He slipped and fell flat on his back, cracking his head on the ground. Flares of pain swirled through his vision and his ears rang. The fall may have saved him once, but now that he was on the ground, there was nowhere else for him to go. He shut his eyes and waited for the spear to skewer him.

But, the soldier simply shuffled on, grim and silent and blank. Something glinted silver but oddly orange-tinted. A bracelet, maybe? The soldier passed by Gan without a second glance.

Gan tried to stand, but slipped again on something slick and warm that smelled of copper. Blood. Blood *everywhere.* It ran through the cracks in the cobblestones, flowing from...

"*No!*"

The garden.

Gan scrambled to his feet and hobbled to the garden, his equilibrium thrown off by his splitting headache and the icy fear of what he would find.

The first thing he saw were the butterflies—stark and vibrant against the blood coating the cobblestones. Their wings had been mangled—flattened against the stones and fluttering faintly with the breeze.

The children had gone to check on their butterflies.

Gan put the back of his hand to his teeth to keep from crying out. All of them were there save for the youngest, Ro. All completely still and surrounded by mangled butterflies. Bile rose in his throat. Who had done this? Who could do something so horrific—so *evil?* They had all been so young. *Too* young. Had Salaith really—

And then he saw her, stretched before their little forms like a shield. A woman crowned in fiery curls.

"*Merra!*" The scream that broke through Gan's chest was a feral, haunting thing that resonated so deeply in his body that nearly all sensation left him. All he could see was the deep pool of blood around her, nearly as scarlet as her hair. He ran to her, but each step was not enough. He had to be faster. Stronger. Maybe he could save her if he could make up even just a few extra moments.

He collapsed next to her—his knees immediately drenched in her blood—and cradled her to him. She bled from a wound in her stomach, her skin so pale against the red stain that she looked nearly translucent. "Merra? *Merra?*" His tongue was lead in his mouth, his jaw and lips numb. She couldn't be...They had a *life* to live together—to watch every sunrise and sunset as silver traced its way through their hair. To laugh and to cry and to work and to fall asleep in each other's arms every night. They had made those promises to each other the moment they exchanged their humble copper rings. And now, those rings were slick with blood and tears. "*Merra!*"

Her eyelashes fluttered, and then she opened her eyes. Gan sobbed in relief. He had never seen something so beautiful.

Merra drew in a breath that gurgled in her throat and coughed up blood. She curled her fist in Gan's tunic. "Gan...Gan, the children..."

Gan shook his head, the bile—the *horror*—returning. He took her face in his hand and kissed her forehead. "You did what you could for them."

It took her a moment to register what he'd said. When she did, she clenched her teeth and tears spilled down her cheeks. A sob wrenched from her body, followed by more coughing.

Gan put one arm beneath her knees while the other wrapped beneath her shoulders. "We're getting you to a healer."

She shook her head even as another attack wracked her body.

"*Merra!* I am getting you *help!*"

"There's no point," she said, her voice already weakening. She put a hand to Gan's cheek and gave him a sad smile. "There's no...point."

"Merra, I am going to find a way to *save* you. I'm your *husband*. I am supposed to protect you!"

"You have. You have been nothing but a good and faithful husband." She ran her thumb along his jawline. "And now there's someone who needs you more."

"What are you talking about? I'm not leaving you!"

"Eden and...Ro are alive. They left the garden to change Ro's shoes. She'd come looking for you."

Gan saw the life draining from Merra's face and could do nothing but watch. Tears dripped from the end of his nose. "I should have been here."

She shook her head. "There was no escaping them. Lord Sedick came to the courtyard and said something, and they just...*attacked*. This was Osmen. I know it." She took Gan's hand in hers. "You can't let him win. If he gets to Ro and Eden's unborn child, it's all over."

"Merra, I've already told you, I'm not leaving you."

"She's your friend, Gan, and that boy needs you." Her voice was so weak now Gan could barely hear it. She brushed her lips across his knuckles. "I love you. *Promise* me."

Gan choked back the lump of helplessness that threatened to strangle him. "I pr—"

But she slipped away before he could finish. Her fingers dropped from his as she let out a final shuddering breath. Her eyes fell closed, never to open again.

Gan's world stopped. All the air fled from his lungs. His vision narrowed only to Merra. He saw the dimple in her cheek that had first caught his eye. Saw the scar above her left eyebrow from when she had accidentally hit her head on the corner of their table while picking up a rogue potato. He saw the smile lines around her eyes— the lips he had kissed a thousand times. A whole, happy life carved into one face.

And now it was gone. Forever.

Gan wanted to sit with her for eternity—to weep and grieve and let the earth swallow him up. But Merra, in her infinite goodness, would not let him. She had given him one final job to do. And he would make sure it was done.

"I promise."

Gan laid Merra on the ground, crossing her hands over her chest. He took a strand of her hair and put it in his pocket. With a last parting look and sob, he ran to the castle, praying that he wouldn't fail her again.

GAN'S LIMBS were like lead as he dragged himself through the palace hallways. His head ached, and his heart and mind grated against their shattered pieces. Around every corner he saw a shock of red hair or felt a phantom touch on his forearm—heard familiar whispers in Merra's voice. But he knew they were lost to him forever now.

And that filled him with feral fury.

It had been unsettlingly easy to get into the palace once he had gotten past the guards. It was as if they were marionettes given one purpose only—to drive everyone out and away from the palace. But why?

Even with the grief still weighing on his shoulders, Gan's mind couldn't stop racing. What was the point of it all? So much bloodshed. So many lives lost. Merra's face swam in his mind.

Bodies littered the white hallways, their blood staining the floor crimson. Servants, loyal friends to the king—not a single one of them had been spared. Gan checked each one for signs of life, but there was nothing. Only their trail of gore as they led directly to the throne room.

Gan inched along, his heart thundering in his chest. That was the only place Osmen could be. What would Gan find there? What would he do when he came face-to-face with the man responsible for Merra's death? His mind raced with all the creative possibilities if he had been younger, larger, and more powerful.

But he was not any of those things. He was just Gan. Just a man that couldn't save his own wife.

But, with Sister Earth as his witness, he would do everything in his power to fulfill his promise to Merra. He owed her at least that much, and a thousand lifetimes over.

Gan slowed as he approached the throne room. Searing adrenaline and icy terror battled through his body. Osmen was there. That monster would be behind that door, and Gan would have to do something about it. He peered into the throne room, expecting Osmen to be draped smugly across the throne. But he was not there. Instead, there was only one man, laid across the steps, gasping as he drowned in his own blood.

Salaith.

Gan crouched, his eyes darting around the room. This felt like a trap. The moment he moved to help the king, someone would dart from the shadows and finish him off. But Gan couldn't see anyone. Just his king dying alone. Biting back his fear, Gan crouched and rushed to Salaith's side.

The hazy light from the skylight above caught the deep murk of Salaith's blood as it stained across his body. He looked at Gan with milky, pain-filled eyes, his hand clenching and unclenching around his sword.

"Osmen," he wheezed. "You were...right."

Gan shook his head. "It was your queen who saw what he could do."

Panic rose in Saliath's face. True fear. "Eden! She and Ro... escaping through...cellars. He's gone to kill...them." He seized Gan by the tunic. "Help! Please. You have to..."

Gan nodded. "I will."

Salaith's eyes began to lose their focus. He sunk deeper to the floor. "Thank you." With great effort, he unbuckled his scabbard and pushed it and his sword to Gan. "Here," he wheezed. "When you find them. My son ought to have...something of his father."

Gan took them, his stomach roiling with turmoil. "I will find them, sire," he said.

"Make sure my son...is a better man than me."

Gan nodded, his hands shaking, and turned to leave. He knew there was nothing else he could do for Salaith now. But, Salaith called him back. "Wait!" He took a shuddering breath, his eyes heavy. "Merra?"

Gan clenched his teeth and shook his head, trying not to let the fresh wave of grief drive him to his knees.

"I'm sorry."

Those were the last words King Salaith spoke. A single, final show of kindness. Maybe Eden really had known a different king than Gan had.

Gan left the throne room, buckling the scabbard around his waist as tight as he could, the belt still loose on his small frame, and turned down the hallway to the cellars. The door was wide open when he reached them, belching acrid smoke.

"No. No! Please, no!" He barreled down the steps. The deeper he went, more smoke billowed up toward him. Gan hardly registered it as he descended, nearly tripping over himself and the sword at his side as he charged into it. The only thing that continued to flash through his mind, even as the smoke filled his lungs and burned his eyes, was Merra's smile. The smile he would never see again. If she hadn't charged him with finding Eden, he would have laid down and died beside her.

When Gan reached the bottom of the steps, hacking and choking, he turned toward the corridor away from the smoke—Eden would have never taken her children into fire like that—but something prickled on the back of his neck. He turned as a figure emerged from the smoke—dirty and covered in blood. And smiling.

Osmen.

Gan froze in place, his eyes locked on the figure that had caused Merra's death. He wanted to rip his throat out—to watch the light fade from his eyes just as Merra's had. But he couldn't make his body move. Salaith's sword hung limp and useless at his side.

But Osmen did not see him. His eyes were glassy, flashing an unusual shade of blue that Gan could even see through the smoke. Osmen brushed past Gan just as wordlessly as the guards had, and mounted the steps two at a time back toward the throne room. The touch sent a shock of pain–of horror and darkness–surging through Gan, as suffocating as the smoke. In that moment, he saw a vision of Eden, dead on the ground, and Ro beneath her. Gan saw the blood on Osmen's sword as he disappeared up the steps, and knew it was true.

Gan's hands shook at his sides. He wanted to collapse–to *break*, to somehow escape the gut-wrenching, soul-shattering reality in which he found himself–but his body refused, and his mind tormented him with the immutable truth. He had been too late. Again.

Drawn on by a morbid sense of finality, Gan dragged himself farther into the smoke.

The fire had come from a wooden hatch in the low ceiling that led into the servants' quarters and kitchens—put there to make shuttling food to and from the cellars more accessible. The wood was completely engulfed, and some had collapsed to the floor. Underneath that burning wreckage, Gan could make out a pair of boots tangled among skirts, and a golden crown. Eden's crown.

Gan's knees finally collapsed, his vision as wavering and dark as the smoke. Merra. Eden. Salaith. He hadn't been able to save anyone. He hadn't even been able to take vengeance on the man that had done all this. Lord Alvace had been right all along. Gan was worthless. He may as well lay down and let the flames take him.

Gan had resigned himself to that fate when a small and delicate sound carried to him over the sound of the flames.

A whimper.

Gan looked up as a small form crawled out from the burning pile of debris. "It's hot," the boy cried weakly, almost incoherently. "Mama, it's *hot.*"

Gan rushed forward, heedless of the burning debris, and scooped the small figure into his arms. Sweet Sister Earth, it couldn't be. He was *alive!* "Ro!"

Ro's eyes fluttered, his little body shaking. Burns—blistered and furious—covered most of his torso. Tears spilled down his cheeks, and he coughed as more smoke swirled around. "Gan," he whimpered. "That man hurt mama." That was the last thing he said before his body went slack. Gan could still see his chest rising and falling.

Gan's thoughts went blank. His body simply moved on its own. He had to get this boy to safety. He *had* to. The weight of his promise to Merra, of Eden's trust, and of Salaith's sword pulled heavy on him. They had to get out. Sister Earth would not spare Ro's life just to make Gan watch him die.

Standing on the wreckage and feeling his boots burn beneath him, Gan pulled himself and Ro up into the kitchen, which was completely engulfed in flames. Gan shielded Ro in his arms and ran through the fire, bashing his shoulder on the main wooden door at the other end until it finally gave way. Through the hallway, around the bodies, avoiding guards. Gan's mind wasn't present for any of it —only his instincts bent on keeping the child in his arms alive.

It was only when the outside air brushed against the blisters on Gan's seared skin that he felt the pain. And with it came the horrible realization that he had no way out. The city would be overrun with guards and people trying to flee. He wouldn't be able to get Ro out. Osmen and Sedick would surely have checkpoints leading out of the city, searching for any survivors from the castle. Even if Gan were to make it past the guards and hide out for a few days, the ferry was certain to be monitored as well. If the long wait without medical attention wouldn't kill Ro first.

Gan's arms tightened around the boy, whose breathing was shallow and labored, punctuated with small whimpers of pain. His heart twisted in his chest, remembering Ro's little grin as he had shown him the bugs in the game forest and medicine bogs. The wonder he had watching the stars. The hugs he gave his older siblings when they fell and scraped their knees. Gan could not let him lose his life before it had even begun.

"Sister Earth, *please*," he wept to himself, his vision swirling with panic and his teeth grinding together. "Give me *something*. Help me save him!"

More glassy-eyed soldiers approached. Gan crouched low behind a stack of crates, his heart hammering. He couldn't let them find Ro.

Luckily, the soldiers passed, but as Gan moved to stand and get away, a shaft of light from a crack in the wall hit his eye. He looked through it, and his face blanched. Out across the ocean, beyond the king's game forest, was a channel of land directly to the mainland. Small and almost invisible—a single golden thread draped across the sea. A channel Gan had never seen before—one that he had only heard about in stories.

The Dragon Scales.

Rays of sunlight broke through the clouds and illuminated pockets of water across the channel as if they were some heavenly messengers. Escape. *Freedom.*

"Sister Earth, *thank you*." Gan clenched one hand around Salaith's sword, ready to fend off anyone that came too close, and darted from his hiding spot, Ro still clutched tightly to him. He inched toward the main gate, every nerve on his body tense and anxious as he waited for guards to leap out at him. His spirit left his body as he turned a corner and came face-to-face with a large, heavily armored guard carrying double-swords at his sides. Gan stumbled back, grabbing for Salaith's sword, but there was no need. The guard stared blankly ahead, off into the streets, like an abandoned play-thing.

Gan rushed away from the man, not wanting to wait around for him to come to his senses. He careened into the courtyard, only to find more guards. All standing silently and unmoving. All looking in the same direction.

Gan heard the clank of weapons and heavy-mail. He turned– looking the same direction as all the mute soldiers. An army of ragged thieves and vagabonds made their way through the streets, grinning as they smashed store fronts and shepherded fleeing people into their clutches. It was the group Osmen had been amassing for months.

Gan cursed. He veered toward the royal stables. If all the guards were like this, then maybe...

By only the fate and grace of the goddess, any soldiers stationed at the stables had abandoned them. Gan commandeered one of the horses, hearing Osmen's army growing steadily closer.

Get out. Get out. GET OUT.

He swung onto the horse, settled Ro in front of him, and burst out of the stables toward the city wall. Cries from Osmen's horde sounded at his appearance, and he heard heavy footsteps coming after him, but he urged the horse ever faster. A sort of weightlessness filled his chest as the earth rumbled beneath his mount. A blessing from Sister Earth–it had to be. The men's voices grew distant behind them.

Osmen's voice, though—amplified with what only could have been magic—followed Gan through the city. "The kingdom of Loralan has suffered long enough," he said, his voice soft and sorrowful, as genuine as fool's gold. "Plague, wars, and starvation have rampaged through our people for centuries, and nothing has been done to stop it. Our royal family has imbibed on our pain and used our broken backs as stepping stones to wealth and comfort. They have sent us to fight their wars and increase their power, while we have gained *nothing*."

The city wall came into view, portions of it crumbling from years of the ocean's abuse. Just beyond those crumbling borders, Gan saw the glint of the Dragon Scales.

"Almost there!" he hissed, spurring the horse forward. It leapt over a crumbling section and into freedom, away from Osmen's gathering horde.

"I have stood by for too long and watched my people suffer. And now I say, no more. A new regime rises. One in which King Salaith, and all those loyal to him, have no place." Osmen continued. "The Lords of the Council are dead, drowned in their sins and killed by their king. And now, Salaith and his family have joined them."

Cries rose up from the city—rough voices that tore through every alleyway. Osmen's horde.

"Long live King Osmen. Long live King Osmen!"

More screams followed–the sounds of Monterro's citizens–and the city blazed with fire.

With heaving, gasping sobs, Gan tucked Ro closer to him. "You're going to stay alive, do you understand?" he told the boy. "I have lost everything to that man, and I will not lose you, too. There's so much life ahead of you, and I will see you back on your rightful throne one day. I swear it."

GAN COLLAPSED outside the swirling mists of the Woods of Desolation. He couldn't see straight. The world swayed around him from pain, hunger, and exhaustion. He had lost track of the hours they had ridden. With every hoofbeat, though, he had watched Ro decline. The boy was so pale. Fevers wracked his little body, and he only took a breath every few seconds. Gan's heart pounded like war drums in his chest as he watched him. No. No. He wouldn't lose him too.

But the darkness of unconsciousness wavered on the edges of Gan's mind. Tired. So tired.

"Help," he croaked to the swirling, unfeeling mist. His body gave out. He had just enough sense to fall backward so that Ro didn't get crushed beneath him, and then the world went dark.

MERRA DANCED in Gan's dreams. Smiling, happy, and alive. Holding Ro on her hip as she wiped dirt off his face. Sunbeams that came from nowhere and everywhere at once shone on her, turning her hair to rubies and transforming her into a goddess of light.

Gan tried to run to her, his heart lurching to his throat, but his feet stayed anchored where he stood.

Merra kissed Ro's forehead and looked at Gan with warm, glistening eyes.

"Take care of him," she said. "Live a long, happy life together. I will wait for you." She set Ro down and he wandered to Gan, grasping his hand.

"Thank you, Gan," Eden said, appearing from the sunlight and standing beside Merra. "Thank you for protecting him."

"Wait!" Gan lunged for Merra, his grip still tight on Ro's hand.

"Bye, Mama," Ro said quietly, waving to Eden.

Gan's fingers slipped through Merra. An inarticulate, broken sound wrenched from his chest.

Tears poured from Merra's eyes, but she smiled, brilliant and beautiful. "Don't you *dare* come back to me until you're older than dirt, do you understand? I expect you to live twice as long, now. For the both of us."

And then she was gone.

GAN'S EYES FLEW OPEN. The first thing they focused on was a single pea vine that had crept in through a windowsill. It sprouted a single red blossom. Merra's favorite.

The memories shuddered through him. He could still feel Merra go limp in his arms. Still see the smoke billowing through the castle. And little Ro.

He stiffened. *Ro.* Where was he?

Gan lurched from the bed he'd been lying on, swaying as lightheadedness overtook him. He coughed, his throat raw and grating with dryness. "Ro!" His voice didn't make it far—weak and wheezing. He stumbled past an assortment of potions, herbs, and plants perched on every available surface, smelling so strong Gan's head swam. Where was he? How had they gotten here?

And *where was Ro?*

He burst out of the small room he had been sleeping in and into a small dining area and kitchen. Two other doors lined the walls, but still no Ro. Gan's heart thundered in his ribcage. Not already. He couldn't have lost him already. Not after escaping Monterro. Not after making it nearly to the Golden Grove. He had promised...

"*Ro!*" Gan tripped over a chair and it fell with enough force to wake the dead. Gan ignored it and burst into the nearest door.

"Pipe down!" an elderly elf snapped as she glowered at him from inside. A warm, crackling fire illuminated her frizzy white hair and long drooping ears in an amber glow. "You shouldn't be out and about yet."

But Gan didn't hear her. He only had eyes for Ro, who was laying on a table as the elf administered to him. Breathing. *Alive.*

Gan sank against the door, passing a hand over his eyes. "Thank the goddess."

"We've heard word of what happened in Monterro," the elf said grimly, beckoning Gan further into the room. "Some of our villagers found you outside the Desolate Woods on their way to deliver the news. By the way you and he are dressed, I would assume he is the last of the royal family?"

Gan hesitated in answering, which only seemed to confirm the answer. She nodded. "Do not fret. You will be safe here." The elf dabbed a salve on the furious burns along Ro's torso. Ro didn't make a sound—didn't even move. He just stared wordlessly at nothing.

Gut wrenching and throat constricted, suddenly feeling wholly inadequate, Gan crept closer. "Ro?" he asked softly.

Ro didn't respond.

Gan looked to the elf with worry.

She sighed. "He's been this way since he woke up," she said, her voice distant and hurting. She put her salve away and carefully wrapped a stack of folded bandages around Ro. It didn't take her long. He was so small. She placed the back of her knuckles to his forehead—swept some of his dark, downy hair away from his eyes. "Children should never have to suffer like this."

Gan inched closer, his whole body trembling. "Will he live?"

"These burns are severe, but his fever has finally broken, and I've managed to stave off any infection for now. He needs to regain strength, though, and that is up to him to do."

She tied off the end of the bandages and gathered the rest of her supplies. "My name is Hemlock, by the way. Welcome to the Golden Grove." She patted Gan's shoulder and then left them alone.

Gan approached Ro like he would a frightened animal. He had hoped the boy's bright smile—his indomitable happiness—would have stayed. But, he knew better. No one could have escaped Monterro unchanged.

The empty glassiness in Ro's eyes didn't falter when Gan came close, but he held his arms out to be held. Gan picked him up, careful not to jostle his bandages, and held him close. Ro's weight and warmth settled against Gan's chest, heavy, exhausted, and traumatized, and a lump swelled into Gan's throat. Ro was so young. *Too* young to have experienced so much. He just wanted to wrap him up and shield him from the rest of the world forever. But he knew he could not. So, instead, he put a bracing palm on the boy's back and hummed hoarsely in his ear.

Gan eased into Hemlock's rocking chair by the fire. Ro nestled his head on Gan's shoulder. They sat like that in grief-stricken quiet for a long time.

"It hurts," Ro whispered.

Gan rubbed Ro's back. "I know," he said, his voice husky at the injustice of it all. "Burns are painful, but we're going to get you medicine and—"

"No," Ro interrupted, shaking his head. "On the inside." Gan felt droplets of Ro's tears fall onto his collarbone. "We don't get to see our families anymore, do we?"

Gan placed his trembling hand on Ro's head, stroking his hair, his body numb. He rocked back and forth in the rocking chair, trying to fight back his own tears and failing miserably. "No," he said. "We just have each other, now."

"Okay," Ro whispered, the tears in his voice evident. "I miss them, though."

"Me too," Gan choked out, wishing to feel Merra's touch one last time.

They stayed that way long into the night.

HEMLOCK'S HOME was silent for days. After that first night, Ro hadn't spoken a single word. Gan couldn't blame him. Hemlock had gone about her work, efficient and kind without prying too much into Gan's and Ro's inner thoughts. Just as well. If not for constantly worrying over Ro, Gan knew he would have sunk too deeply into his thoughts and memories, and, in his current state, that would destroy him.

So, they were quiet, each carrying their separate griefs, until Gan awoke one morning to the sound of chatter and squeals.

He furrowed his brow and poked his head into the kitchen. Hemlock wasn't there. "Hello?"

Another peal of laughter. From Ro's room.

Gan padded to the door and inched it open. Was Ro making noises in his sleep?

When Gan peered inside, though, Ro was not sleeping. Instead, Ro watched wide-eyed as a pudgy little girl with dark hair and pointed ears babbled to him, offering him rocks from her pockets and flowers missing half their petals. Ro actually laughed when she offered him a disgruntled, mildly squashed toad from inside her cloth diaper. The sound washed over Gan like sunshine over a frozen pond—cracking the hollow, dead parts of himself to reveal his beating heart beneath.

The little girl arranged all of her treasures at Ro's feet and then clambered onto the bed with him, planting a sloppy kiss on his forehead with a proclamation of "All better!" before going back to playing.

Gan was so enthralled by the moment that he hardly heard Hemlock approach from behind.

"That's Aspen," she told him quietly, smiling as she watched the children play. "Her mother generally drops her off with me while she's running errands. Ro's been healing so well, though, that I requested she make an extra, special visit." She patted Gan's arm. "It looks like they're going to be all right."

Gan smiled, realizing his cheeks were wet as he watched Ro, marveling at the light that had come back to the boy's face. A weight lifted from Gan's chest. There was still a world of love and kindness. A world where happiness wasn't a fool's errand, and where children could still be children. He almost swore he felt a hand slip into his, and a kiss brush his cheek.

"I think you're right," he wept.

WAR AGAIN DESCENDS

War descends anew on Loralan's tired land
The king and queen o'erturned.
The men who stormed the castle keep
Blame magic for their deeds.
The words of hypocrites are believed
And hatred rears its sleeping head.

The magic-born are torn asunder
'Til they find ground beneath their feet
They defend and soon attack
And victory retreats where none can follow.
A child cries for her mother.
The land cries for relief.

No prayer is answered
No wish is heard.
And the kingdom stains scarlet
From the lives of its kin.

RING OUT THE BELLS

The bells of war
Toll for us all.
To arms – to battle! – we go
For what we fight we do not know
To our King this all is for!

Ring out the bells
For the saints and the sinners.
Ring out the bells
For the lives that are lost.
Come join the game
Where there are no winners,
If you're willing to pay the cost.

The bells of war
Ring out our deaths.
Hundreds – thousands? – we do not know.
Only to battle we go
To settle a nameless score.

Ring out the bells
For the saints and the sinners.
Ring out the bells
For the lives that are lost.
Come join the game
Where there are no winners,
If you're willing to pay the cost.

The bells of war
Will call to you
As they have come for them – for me.
And ready decrees the King you'll be
To settle in with the gore.

Ring out the bells
For the saints and the sinners.
Ring out the bells
For the lives that are lost.
Come join the game
Where there are no winners,
If you're willing to pay the cost.

The bells of war
Need not ring out
Peace can – must! – be found
Lest we find ourselves deep in the ground
The world deceased for ever more.

But should peace be a burden
And bloodshed a friend
Then you have chosen your end.

Ring out the bells
For the saints and the sinners.

A. L. LORENSEN

Ring out the bells
For the lives that are lost.
Come join the game
Where there are no winners,
If you're willing to pay the cost.

SHADOW WALKER'S CURSE

Cowards never sleep
Haunted by lives they ended
In their fear's retreat.

Pariahs walk free
Chained by shadow; thrown aside
Home to never be.

Shadow walkers all
Ever cursed by courage failed
Trav'ling loveless roads.

WHEN ALL IS AT AN END

To the shadows
We give our fears
They hold them
Caress them
And give them place outside ourselves
That we may sleep and dream

To the sunlight
We give our hope
It cradles it
Blesses it
And gives it place outside ourselves
That we may dream and fly

All is right
And in its place
Though fear may poison dreams
And fear may shatter with broken wings

Evil bares its wicked fangs for a season
'Fore peace lulls it to its rest.
All must happen for a reason
For sweet cannot be savored
Without knowledge of the bitter.

All will end
As all things do
Pain will inflict its last wounds
Love will paint them with healing scars
Sorrow will not last forever
For we are determined to nurture joy
Where none should grow.

Toil to rest
Grief to gratitude
Sorrow to hope
Anguish to love
'Til all the world
Is ripe with healing
And sighs its final, peaceful breath.

I will watch for that day to come
When all the world is quiet
Its yearning for peace fulfilled.
And then I shall lay myself to rest.
I'll dream without fear
I'll hope without tether
And thank the heavens
I lived to tell their tales.

ALSO BY A. L. LORENSEN

For Evergreens and Aspen Trees: The Songs of Loralan, Book 1

Of Starlit Blade and Hallowed Flames: The Songs of Loralan, Book 2

ACKNOWLEDGMENTS

This book has been on quite the journey. It started out as a collection of poetry I put together for an Instagram challenge, and was technically my first body of strictly my own work that got published. Unfortunately, my "due diligence" was not as thorough as it should have been, and the company I originally published that poetry through was not as honest as I had hoped. But, we live and we learn.

The truly beautiful thing about that frustrating experience was that it gave me a kick in the pants to actually go on and publish my debut novel, *For Evergreens and Aspen Trees*. I loved that feeling of holding my own book in my hands. I still do.

So, I should first thank that shady publisher for making parts of this book exist in the first place. It feels good to finally, fully reclaim it, along with adding in new short stories to make it even better than before.

A MASSIVE thank you, as always, to my editor, Aria Carpenter. She sat with my as I frantically finished drafting some of these stories and calmly edited as I went. I got editing services and moral support for the price of one! Also, just thank you for being a stand-up, amazing human in general.

Thank you to Phi Pilgrim for keeping me in check, on task, and for having unfailing belief in me. I am still so incredibly grateful that the stars aligned and brought us to work together.

Ryan, you are the most amazing husband I have ever had (and the only one I ever will have). Thank you for believing in me, supporting me, and encouraging me to rest when I need to. This book would not exist without you.

A huge thank you to all my other close friends and family. You may not feel like you had a hand in creating these stories, but you are the people that inspire me and motivate me. You have shaped my writing by shaping me, and I can never thank you enough for that.

And, to my readers, thank you for being here. You are more numerous, lovely, and amazing than I could have ever expected. You make every moment of being an author worth it. Thank you for giving me that gift.